Land of the Unknown: Egress

Hills of Hell
Thead
Riveren
Dunes
of the
Dead

Hills of Hell

Rebel
Camp II

Land of the Unknown:

Egress

Mario A Hernandez

For information address:
Oprelle Publications,
236 Twin Hills Rd.
Grindstone, PA 15442.

FIRST EDITION

ISBN: 979-8-9899015-2-4

In dedication to Agustin Bizarron,
"May the path you carved lead us to new heights."

Also a special thanks to Omar Bizarron,
Nora, Mario, Ivan, and Gina Hernandez
for your endless support.

CHAPTER ONE

Thoughts of banshees, werewolves, vampires, cyclops, and various other monsters and creatures fill Jonathan's mind as he struggles to look busy during class. Faintly, he can hear his teacher lecturing about some ancient history. However, Jonathan isn't interested in that history. He is only interested in the history of the worlds of magic; magic which once possessed this Earth but later faded away.

Jonathan has his history book open on his wooden desk, but under the history book, he has another book—a much more interesting one. He glances up quickly to check if his teacher is distracted. Once he realizes that she is, he brings the hidden book out from behind his textbook. The black cover of the book has this rough texture, almost as if it were made from the scales of a reptile. The ancient book cover feels dry but somehow also moist. This is the Book of Embers, and it is one of the many ancient books of magic that Jonathan possesses. This particular book is an encyclopedia for every creature and monster that lives in the world known as Domum and is part of a small collection of ancient magical texts that Jonathan's father left him.

Jonathan did not know his father; he died not long after Jonathan's birth. Jonathan has been raised by his uncle and aunt since then, and he knows very little about his father. In fact, his only real connection to his father is the ancient texts that he left for Jonathan.

The books are not from this world. Jonathan found that out when he quickly realized no records of these books exist on Earth. At first, he thought they were pieces of really detailed fiction or even some Lord of the Rings fanfiction. Somehow, Jonathan always believed that these books were real accounts of a magical world that got lost in time, and he is the only one with knowledge of that world. There are five books in total, of varying styles… some of the books are guides or encyclopedias, while others seem to have spells or accounts of wars.

The Book of Embers has always interested Jonathan the most because it seemed to give the most detail about this fantastical world. The book gives insightful details about the creatures and monsters of a world called Domum. He has probably read this book the most; he loves taking in every detail of every named creature and fantasizing about how gruesome these creatures would actually be in reality.

Jonathan's fascination with these books has always bothered his aunt and uncle, as he seems to take more of an interest in learning about Domum than he does about anything on Earth. But his aunt and uncle have never stopped him from reading these books despite their obvious disapproval of them. They just play it off as their nephew being obsessed with fantasy. However, these books aren't just fantasy for Jonathan; they are much more like reality. These books give him a warm feeling as if he was reading a letter from a loved one. Somewhere deep down, he truly believes with every ounce of his spirit that this world that he reads about is real.

"Jonathan!"

Jonathan's skeleton nearly jumps out of his skin when he realizes that the entire class is staring at him. Jonathan quickly realizes he must have been called on by his teacher and was lost in fantasy. His face quickly blushes with embarrassment as the entire class laughs at him. The laughs tend to mute themself into the background—all but one of them. One obnoxiously violent and loud laugh sticks out to Jonathan—that of Adrian Brady. Adrian is a short yet stout teenager with slicked-back greaser hair and the plainest clothes ever. His laugh stands out because it is backed with a real distaste for Jonathan. Adrian and Jonathan have known each other since grade school, yet Adrian has constantly mocked Jonathan. Adrian has always preyed on Jonathan's unusual obsession with the occult. Adrian stares directly at Jonathan and makes a choking gesture, which brings Jonathan's attention back to reality.

"I'm sorry about that, Mrs. Davis. I might have gotten distracted."

"Care to share what part of the textbook has you so distracted?"

Jonathan's face turns the color of a ripe tomato.

"Well, what is it?"

Jonathan does not respond.

"Well, what book are you reading?"

Jonathan does not respond but lets out a nervous smile.

"Jonathan, if you do not tell me, I will just confiscate it."

"It's the Book of Embers," Jonathan says as he gives up.

"I've never heard of it before, but I'm sure it has nothing to do with American history, so please put it away."

"Of course, you haven't heard of it, Mrs. Davis. It's one of the many satanic books that Jonathan owns," Adrian says as the entire class erupts into laughter.

"That's enough, everyone. Let's all get back to work." Jonathan lets out a sigh of relief as he thinks he got away with his act.

"Jonathan, please put the book away and see me after class."

Jonathan closes the Book of Embers and returns to the much more complicated world of American history.

* * *

Jonathan sits anxiously in his seat as the rest of the students file out of the classroom. Mrs. Davis gets up from her seat, sits on her desk, and lets out a sigh.

"Jonathan, how many times am I going to have to confiscate one of these books from you?"

"I'm sorry, Mrs. Davis, I truly am. It won't happen again."

"You said that last time. If I catch you reading anything but our textbook, I will lock them up, and your aunt or uncle will have to come to pick it up."

"Please, don't do that."

"Then, please do not make me do it."

"You're a smart kid, Jonathan, you really are, but you need to get your head out of your fantasy world and focus on reality."

"I'm sorry, Mrs. Davis, I really am."

"What is this book that causes you so much trouble anyway?"

"It's called the Book of Embers," he says quietly.

"Oh, I'm afraid I have not heard of it."

"Well, you wouldn't have, it's an… uh… one of a kind."

"Does it really involve black magic?"

"No, it doesn't. It's just fiction," Jonathan says defensively.

"Very well. Well, please keep it away during class time." She then directs her eyes to the door.

"Will do, Mrs. Davis." Jonathan jumps out of his chair and almost runs out of the class.

Jonathan walks into the seemingly empty hallway to see his best friend, Stephen, standing at their adjacent lockers. Stephen is wearing his typical torn jeans with a dirty gray t-shirt. The nature of his clothes fits Stephen's punk-rock look. However, Jonathan knows he dresses that way because he can't afford nice clothes and not because of his musical taste. Although they both like the same music, their clothing separates them, as Jonathan always has the nicest and newest clothes in school. Their financial backgrounds have always been an awkward point of contention between the two, although they never mention it. Stephen's eyes light up as he notices Jonathan.

"Dude, what the heck?"

"Sorry, sorry… Mrs. Davis held me back again."

"Again? That's like the hundredth time this month! You need to get better at hiding it. You should leave it with me."

"What? No way I would let you keep your greasy fingers on this beauty," Jonathan says as he demonstrates the book.

"Yeah, man, whatever. That book is too important to fall into the hands of Mrs. Davis, so just be more careful."

"You got it, boss."

"Yeah, imagine the chaos Mrs. Davis could bring upon the world if she knew all about the elder magic and American history."

"You're an idiot."

"I'm just saying, with knowledge like that, she could rule this entire planet."

"Alright, Fen, that's enough speculation. Let me get my jacket so we can leave this dump."

Jonathan and Stephen walk home from school every day. They both live on the south side of town. Not that it makes the walk fun, as the trail is nothing special; similar suburban homes lined up like dominoes. The homes are perfectly far enough from the factories that burn the otherwise crisp oxygen. Street after street, they all look the same; they're just dull-colored homes, surrounded by grey cement and cars. Jonathan always mentioned how grey and boring their town is. They both have the same distaste for this boring grey town. The only interesting thing on the way home is a park… not an official park, but rather a huge patch of grass and trees with a makeshift dirt path. Since the inception of their friendship, Jonathan and Stephen have loved this area of town, as it has always seemed to hold the entirety of the town's natural color that was sorely missing from the rest of the town.

This clearing holds more trees than the rest of the town. With trees of various sizes and colors, Jonathan and Stephen always cut through this area as it had something that they were both fans of – the natural world. They could never fully explain their love for this patch of grass and trees, but they liked the way it reminded them of the world that they read about in Jonathan's books of magic. All the books seem to come from authors from a world or worlds where the natural world reigned supreme. In those stories, the humans were connected with the world and respected it; in turn, the natural world blessed the humans with pure natural magic.

As they walk through a particularly shady part of the area, Stephen takes note of the warm feeling that is always accompanied by this area despite the weather. This same feeling somehow radiated from the books of magic, but Jonathan could never understand why.

"Yeah, I always feel it too. It's weird because the trees cover most of the sunlight, yet it feels as if the sun is shining on us directly."

"Yes, exactly! Almost as if the trees are keeping us warm."

"Ha! Warm trees?" Jonathan says with a smirk.

"Hey, we both believe in the orcs and crazy stuff from those books, yet you don't believe trees can give us warmth."

"I mean sure, but you and I have read the books several times, and never have they mentioned anything about living trees. This isn't Lord of the Rings."

"Good thing it isn't because if it was, I'm sure you'd qualify as an orc."

"Better than a living tree."

They stare at each other and then burst out into laughter.

The cover of the trees begins to fade as the pair leave the shady area and descend into the small clearing that rounds out the park. As they continue down the path, they notice a homeless man in the distance. As Jonathan and Stephen get closer to the man, who is now walking towards them, they move slightly off the dirt path so that he may pass. As the homeless man gets closer, Jonathan begins to tense up; his aunt always warns him about the homeless in this area, saying that this area used to be a homeless camp full of druggies and alcoholics until the city kicked them out. In fact, Jonathan wasn't supposed to be walking through here even though it's a shortcut to home. His aunt and uncle made him promise to take the long industrial way home. Jonathan begins to take a mental photo of the homeless man as he passes by; he's wearing a dirty and torn black and white suit with a red vest. Stephen senses Jonathan's unease and stops talking as they pass the man. Once they pass the man, Stephen addresses the situation.

"What happened, man, you okay?"

"Yeah, I'm fine. I just zoned out."

"Did that guy scare you or something?"

"What? No. I was just thinking about something."

"You sure seemed nervous around him."

"I just got a weird feeling from him, that's it."

"Okay, man, sure," Stephen says, unconvinced.

"I just… I have seen that man before so many times. There were a couple of times where I could have sworn he was stalking me."

"You think he would follow you?"

"Maybe. I don't know, maybe I'm just being paranoid."

After a bit more walking through grey suburban streets, the pair come to the train tracks. The train tracks are old and were put here when the town was first founded, but it ironically now serves as a border that separates the lower and higher parts of town. Stephen lives in the lower part of town where the homes are older and are practically falling apart, while Jonathan lives in the newer, cleaner upper side of town. Although they are friends, they have always had a bit of distance between them when it comes to their financial backgrounds. Jonathan was constantly told by his aunt and uncle to avoid that part of town, especially the many homeless, drunks, and druggies who lived in that area. Although his aunt and uncle didn't mean Stephen, he knew they were talking about the people who lived around him.

"Alright, man, I'll see you tomorrow."

"See ya," Stephen replied.

Jonathan stands still as he watches his best friend crossing the train tracks into his neighborhood. He knows how much Stephen hates being home; although he doesn't always talk about it, Jonathan knows Stephen's home life isn't the best.

"Stephen!" Jonathan says as he jogs over to join him. Stephen's eyes widen as he turns to see his best friend crossing the train tracks.

"Dude, what the hell are you doing?"

"You should come over for a bit."

"What? Are you sure? I mean, aren't your aunt and uncle home?"

"No, they were going out after work, so I have the house to myself."

"I don't know, man, I should really get home."

"Come on, Fen, I'm sure you have nothing to do."

"I don't know. I'd like to, but I shouldn't."

"Come on, live a little." Jonathan nudges Stephen.

"Alright, fine. I mean, I guess I have time."

"Of course you have time."

Stephen immediately feels out of place as they stroll through the pristine houses with new cars parked in each of their driveways. Stephen loves spending time with Jonathan, but he has never actually been to Jonathan's house. Not because of Jonathan but what might happen if his aunt and uncle find him.

There has always been this awkward tension whenever Jonathan mentions his aunt and uncle around Stephen. Although they have never said it explicitly, Stephen knows that they do not like him and do not approve of his friendship with Jonathan.

All of Stephen's fears disappear when they start playing video games together. Stephen feels happy in the unknown house. They played video games for what seemed like a few minutes. It wasn't until Jonathan went to the restroom that Stephen noticed that it was dark out.

"I need to go!" Stephen says, standing up in a rush.

"Dude, are you okay?"

"Yeah, I just need to go," Stephen says as he grabs his belongings and runs from the house.

Stephen frantically turns the loose doorknob as he rushes into his house. Stephen feels the anger as he walks into the house; his father is holding a bottle while leaning against the wall, struggling to stand. His eyes are unfocused, but he slowly looks up to notice Stephen. It takes him a few seconds to make sense of the situation in his head.

"You barely getting home?" he spits through the stench of alcohol in his breath. Stephen stares back in response.

"Did you just get home, boy?" His dad is now staring directly at him while his drunken eyes wander. Stephen still does not respond.

"Answer me!" he yells, grabbing Stephen by the face.

"Yes," Stephen says without making eye contact.

"Yes, what? Answer me with respect, boy!"

"Yes, sir," Stephen says quickly.

His dad pushes him away. "You know you need to be home to help with your grandma. Where the hell were you?"

"I know, I'm sorry. I lost track of time."

Stephen's dad looks back at him, surprised. He had not expected an answer.

"I had to leave work early because you lost track of time. That's money out of my pocket!"

"I'm sorry, it was an honest mistake," Stephen says while looking down at the floor.

"Get out of my face, I've had enough of you today."

"But, Dad," Stephen says as he steps forward.

His expression hardens as he says, "Get out of my face."

"Dad, please, I have homework to do."

"Get out of my face!" He throws the bottle towards the wall. Stephen reacts quickly and ducks—the bottle shatters against the wall. Stephen stares back in disbelief. Stephen runs up the stairs to his room; as he is running away, he can hear his father mumble something toxic under his breath.

Stephen is angry and confused but also scared. This is not the first time this has happened, and it surely won't be the last. After staying secluded in his room for some time, he comes out into the hallway once he no longer hears his father talking drunkenly. Stephen tiptoes down the creaky stairs as he hears nothing but the television. Once he reaches the final step, he takes a deep breath and steps forward into the living room. The old furniture gives the room this wet smell. The living room, like the rest of the house, is small. Stephen's grandma is sitting on the only couch, staring blankly at the flashing pictures on the television. His father is lying on the other couch seemingly passed out from exhaustion from working long hours or from the liters of alcohol pounding in his head. Stephen takes a long look at his father. Most children look up to their father as a role model; at one point Stephen did, but at a young age, he quickly understood that his father was a terrible man and an even worse father. He is the illegitimate father of many children, and Stephen just happens to be the one he got stuck with. Stephen begins to cry as he stares at the mess that is his father, the only real family he has. The tears are born not just of sorrow but also of anger. He has a connection to his father like any child does, but he hates him for everything that he isn't. Stephen turns to his grandmother, who is still blankly staring at the television. She has not even noticed that he has been standing there or any of the commotion from earlier. He stares at the vulnerable woman. He does not feel any remorse toward her. In fact, he feels sorry for her; she has been like this for much of his youth. Stephen's grandmother lost herself long ago, and she still believes Stephen is an infant and that her son is still happily married to Stephen's mother, who would be his dad's first wife. In a way, Stephen envies her; she has this perfect perception of the world and reality, and to her, nothing can change that. Stephen steps closer to her and gives his grandmother a kiss on the forehead; she doesn't smile but looks directly at him.

"You're home already, David?" She then turns back to

the ever-playing television. That is one of the only three sentences she says. He takes one last look at his grandmother, and then he turns his back on his family. With one deep breath and an everlasting gasp, he runs. He runs out of the house that has housed nothing but his sadness. Stephen doesn't think about where he is going to go; he just runs wherever his legs carry him.

Stephen came to the only place he could think of—the clearing that he and Jonathan walked through. It was a warm place despite being dark out, and it provided him with a sense of comfort that his home had not provided in a while. While standing there in the darkness of the moonlight, Stephen is overcome with emotions and begins to cry. This isn't the first time his father has tried to hurt him, and it certainly won't be the last time. Stephen was quite literally counting the days until he could leave for college, hopefully in some other part of the world. Stephen knew he put himself in a bad spot by going over to Jonathan's house. In a strange way, Stephen was mad that Jonathan invited him over, but that was a ridiculous way to think; Jonathan was his best friend, and he never meant any harm. However, deep down, Stephen had some animosity, or rather jealousy, toward his best friend. Stephen hated that he could never go home—not in the same way that Jonathan could.

Stephen ran to the only place that he felt any comfort in, and that was the park. The moon was full and was lighting up the entirety of the park. Stephen's emotions seemed to have calmed themselves as soon as he arrived. That familiar, indescribable, warm feeling comforted him. Stephen sulked in the moonlight and thought over everything. His mind wanders back to his home… is he making the right decision? Should he just go back home and rethink this in the morning with a clear head? No, that wasn't the answer. His home hasn't felt like home in years. Should he go with Jonathan? His aunt and uncle wouldn't like it, but surely, they would understand this time given the circumstances. Or would they turn him away? These thoughts and many more wrestled each other in Stephen's head as he pondered what to do or where to go.

"Excuse me, are you lost?" The voice startles the entranced boy. Stephen breaks out of his trance and freezes in place. If this was his father and he'd found him, then this would be a full-on disaster. But the voice, although cold, was not of his father. Stephen turns around slowly to face the cold mysterious voice. He turns to find an older homeless man. But not just any homeless man; the same homeless man that they walked by earlier. This is the first time Stephen has ever really studied the man up close, and he is now realizing how much this man stands out. The homeless man has a full head of thinning grey hair and piercing blue eyes. He has a full grey goatee that hides his small mouth. He has a scar that goes across the left side of his face. He is wearing a dress shirt that looks older than him and a sharp red waistcoat, but upon further examination, the waistcoat looks like it may have been painted or dyed red. In a strange way, the man looks like some homeless magician.

"How long have you been here?" Stephen takes a few steps back.

"Here? In this park?" the bum says as he looks around the park.

"No, how long have you been watching me?"

"I just found you."

"Do you live here?" Stephen gestures to the park.

"No, I don't really have a home." The man chuckles.

Stephen says nothing; he just stands there, watching the man blankly staring back.

"You've been watching me and my friend for a while. I've noticed you. Every time we walk through here after and before school, I see you. Sometimes close by, sometimes from behind a tree. But there is no doubt that we see you every day. I don't know what your obsession with us is, but you need to stop."

"Stephen, I am not stalking you," the man says seriously.

"Wait! How do you know my name!?" Stephen shouts as he takes a few more steps back. The old man makes a small comment to himself.

"Yes, I have been following you and your friend. But only because I've been tasked by my superior."

"Your superior?"

"Yes, I am sure you will know the mage Magiya."

Stephen's entire body goes cold. That sentence seemingly comes to life and cripples his body. His mind wanders to every corner of the universe, trying to make sense of the situation as his body stands there in complete and utter shock.

"Hello? Stephen?"

"You mean the mage from the books?"

"Yes, exactly. He sent me here for the next mage. He believes it to be you or your friend."

"Wait, how do you know him? Who are you?"

"I'm Joseph Skrinner. I am a member of the Red Realm Rebellion. Magiya sent me here to find the next mage."

"The Red Realm is real?"

"Yes, all of what you've read in your friend's books is

true."

"And you think I'm the next mage for the rebellion?"

"I don't think anything… oddly enough, that's my problem. But Magiya believes so."

"You're telling me I'm the next mage for the Myronids, the protectors and users of light magic?"

"Uh, yes, didn't I make that clear?" Skrinner says sarcastically.

Stephen looks at the many trees surrounding them, then down at the moist grass, and then up at the bright moon. He then sets his eyes on the man standing before him, claiming to be from the same worlds that he and Jonathan have read about for the longest time. Worlds full of magic, magical creatures, and monsters. His whole life, the stories from those books were an escape… fantasies to help him escape his bitter reality. But now there is standing proof that all of the fantasy is real. And not just real, but that same world is calling to him, begging him to join it. "I don't believe you," Stephen says to the dismay of Skrinner.

"What do you think—I just know these very intricate details about your friend's magical books?"

Stephen has no response to that reasoning.

"Look, Stephen, I don't have much time to waste here, and frankly, I hate the stench of this realm. Once, it used to be full of natural beauty, but your kind destroyed all that. So, either you come with me to the Red Realm or stay here, but decide quickly."

"Show me something to prove you're telling the truth."

"What, would you like me to pull a bunny out of my imaginary hat?"

"No, but I want… no, NEED you to prove that you're real."

"If you want me to show you some magic trick, kid, I can't. I don't have magical abilities like that. I was a magician, but I am no mage. The only proof I have is this."

Skrinner reaches into his vest, pulls out a brown bag, and opens it. He takes out a glowing red orb; he holds it out towards Stephen while giving it a little shake. There is a red liquid inside the gel-like orb, and it moves around constantly.

"Do you know what this is?" Skrinner cocks his eyebrow.

"Is it a traveling orb?"

"Technically, yes. But no one calls it that anymore; simply orb will do."

"So, you aren't a Myronid then if you need the orb."

"Kid, I failed that trial years ago. But no, I am not. I tried to be, but what can I say? The Myronids hate handsome applicants like me."

"You're full of personality, Joseph."

"That is Skrinner to you, kid. I may not be a Myronid, but I do possess magical potential, and I am a high-ranking Rebellion Commander."

"That explains it."

"Explains what?"

"Why you feel so familiar to me."

"Pardon?" Skrinner asks, genuinely curious.

"Whenever you are close by, I get this warm feeling from you. I am not sure what it is; it's almost like an instinct. But I get it from certain people, things, and even some places."

"You never made the realization of what that is?"

"Should I have?"

"You seem pretty knowledgeable about the Red Realm

and the Myronids but missed something so obvious. What you are feeling is magic. Magic radiating from me, magic radiating from this patch of grass and trees. You feel that because the magic within you is reaching out to other sources of magic, trying to connect."

Stephen looks around in wonder at the trees around him. That makes sense; it explains the feeling he gets from the park, from Skrinner, and from the Book of Embers.

"You're right. I believe you.

"About what?"

"Everything, I believe you."

"That's the spirit!" Skrinner says in glee.

"I'm sorry I thought you were some homeless man all this time."

"Insult noted," Skrinner says as he claps his hands together.

"Okay, well, we need to go. Are you ready?"

"Wait, already?"

"Yes, I have people waiting for me on the other side."

"I don't have time to say goodbye or anything?"

"To whom? Your father? He won't care, and your grandmother is too senile to understand anything."

"Wow, thanks for that," Stephen says halfheartedly.

"Hey, I'm just some homeless man," Skrinner says and shrugs as he tosses the red orb ahead of them. The red orb evaporates, and a small portal opens up. The portal expands big enough for them to walk through. The orb transforms into a transworld portal, and it acts as a window that allows people to transfer themselves from one realm to another in a matter of seconds. The portal is red in color, and the edges of it are pulsing, almost as if it is alive. Every couple of seconds, the window pulses as if it has a heartbeat.

Stephen stares deeply into the crimson window as he contemplates leaving. He has always wanted a way out, but not death. He loves life and loves his best friend, as well as his grandma before the sickness took over her mind, but he also loves the memories of his mother before her death. He also loves the fantasy of a life that he created here, but now that same fantasy is calling out to him. Besides that, two of those things are gone; he just hopes that Jonathan can manage without him. He hates leaving his friend alone because Stephen knows what it is like to be alone.

"Are you ready for a new world?" Skrinner steps into the portal. Stephen takes one last look at this little park that has become a symbol of his friendship with Jonathan; the trees, the grass, and the way the moon is. With one last gasping breath and a huge leap of faith, he steps forward into a sea of pulsing red.

Chapter Two

Darkness. Red skies. Walls of a cave oozing blood. Screaming. A loud pulsing heartbeat. A dark figure stands in the middle of the cave that oozes blood. The shadow figure reaches out.

"Jonathan!" Mrs. Davis screams.

Jonathan snaps out of his daydream and awakes to the entirety of the class staring at him. The clique of eyes pierce into his soul.

"Please excuse yourself to the main office; you are being picked up early."

Jonathan gathers his backpack and the failed test which had been mysteriously placed on his desk while he was daydreaming.

Daisy, Jonathan's aunt, picked him up early from school. The entire car ride home was nothing but radio silence. Daisy hoped to talk to Jonathan alone about the situation before getting home, but Jonathan did not make any attempts at a conversation. Stephen went missing a couple of weeks ago. His disappearance took a turn for the worse when Jonathan heard the police say he was more than likely dead. Jonathan wasn't exactly the most popular at school;

most students liked him but never made any real attempts to befriend him since most students found his obsession with magic and the occult off-putting.

When Stephen first went missing, rumors started being spread. Students were saying all sorts of outrageous things like Jonathan murdered Stephen, or Stephen's drunk father killed him, or—the worst of all rumors—that Jonathan used his magic to turn Stephen into a frog or something. Jonathan's love for the weird never got him in trouble before, until the disappearance. Now, in the eyes of everybody from school, he had murdered his best friend as a sacrifice to some demon for magical powers.

They arrive home, and Daisy stops the car. As Jonathan begins to open the door, she stops him.

"Jonathan, wait."

Jonathan holds the door open, then slowly closes it.

"I know how hard things are for you right now, but I need you to understand something. I need you to talk to me or your uncle. You need to speak about what's going on, no matter how much it hurts."

"I will, but I just can't right now. I really just want to be alone," Jonathan replies coldly.

"That's fine; we all grieve differently, but whenever you want to talk just know I am here."

"Grieve… what do you mean grieve?"

"I'm sorry, Jonathan, I didn't mean…"

"Why does everyone keep insisting he is dead?!"

"I'm sorry, Jonathan, I misspoke."

Jonathan sat there in silence. For the past couple of weeks, he has been the only one to deny the rumors that Stephen is dead. When Stephen first disappeared, everyone thought he had run away; it made the most sense. Stephen never had the best home life, and maybe he had just run away in the hopes of finding something better. But then, after weeks of questioning family, friends, and acquaintances, the police assumed he was probably dead. They issued warnings to the local cities, but nothing ever came back. The police were supposedly still searching, but everyone has kind of just accepted that Stephen had run away and that something awful had happened to him. Except for Jonathan – he knows that his best friend is still alive. But despite countless talks with police officers, counselors, and his aunt and uncle, no one put any merit in Jonathan's claims.

Since Stephen's disappearance, Jonathan has been different. He is closed off and really quiet. His academics have started falling, and Jonathan has become more and more involved with his readings. Ultimately, this has led to problems with his aunt and uncle, but mostly his uncle, Erik. Erik has been upset with Jonathan, especially since he made the investigation with the officers so difficult and has been slacking in his studies.

Jonathan follows his aunt into the house. A wave of anger hits them as they enter the home. Erik is standing in the center of the living room with a face as red as a tomato.

"We need to talk."

Jonathan is walking, head down, towards the stairs but then stops on the first step. He slowly walks towards the living room while still facing the floor.

"I received a call from your school again." Jonathan does nothing in response to that.

"Look at me and respond," Erik commands.

"I failed another test," Jonathan mumbles.

"It's okay, there will always be more tests. The important thing is you tried your hardest," Daisy injects.

"No, Daisy, it's not okay. This is the third test he's failed. There's no way he's going to pass any of his classes at this rate."

"You don't understand," Jonathan says.

"Apparently, you're not the one understanding, Jonathan. This is the third exam you've failed. Mrs. Davis told me you're on track to fail the course if you fail the final exam. All those years of hard work and perfect academics could be ruined in a matter of weeks. I am not going to let you do that to yourself."

"I can't do it."

"You can't do what?"

"This… or school, or reading, or anything that we do," Jonathan says, as he finally starts getting some thoughts off his chest.

"It doesn't matter if you can't… you have to, and you will continue to do so."

"No, you don't understand. I can't do this crap anymore!"

Jonathan drops his backpack as a mixture of anger and sadness takes over him.

"You don't talk to me like that."

"I have to, or else you don't listen. Nobody listens."

"What the hell are you talking about? We listen to you. We always do."

"No. You hear me, but you don't listen to me. You both think I am some weird psycho who can't accept that his best friend is dead."

"What are you talking about?"

"I know… I know what you both say about me. I know you both think I'm crazy like everyone else does."

"Why are you saying that?"

"I see the way you both look at me when I say he isn't dead."

"When who isn't dead?"

"Stephen! I see the look in everyone's eyes and the small smirk when I say that. I know everyone thinks I'm just some psycho!"

Erik's head falls into his hand. "Jonathan, you can't keep doing this. Your life can't just stop. Stephen is dead. The funeral is in two days; I can't keep having you tell people he isn't dead, especially at the service."

"Who am I going to tell?"

"What?"

"Hardly anyone is going to show. I don't even know why you both are going; you never liked him."

"Jonathan, don't say that."

"What? I'm just telling the truth. You never liked him."

"Don't shout at me," Erik says sternly.

"You two are the only people I have, and it hurts so much that you don't believe me."

"Jonathan. Stephen is dead. There's no changing that."

"You're wrong," Jonathan says with tears in his eyes.

"Why do you say he isn't dead?"

"I don't know, but I just know. I have a feeling, an instinct when I walk by his locker or the park on the way to school. A feeling I always got from him when he was here."

"You're in denial, Jonathan. Go to your room. I'm not talking about this anymore."

"I'm not going to my room," Jonathan says sternly.

"No more books," Erik says with no hesitation.

"What?"

"Your books, your magic books… give them to me."

"What?! No."

"You want to act like a child. I'm going to treat you like one. Give me the books."

"No, I'm not giving them to you!"

"Go to your room and stay there. Don't come out till your aunt or I come get you."

Jonathan tries to think of something to say, but his lips cannot form any words. With tears in his eyes and a lasting wish, he rushes to his room.

Later that night, Jonathan is sitting in his room thinking about the altercation earlier with his uncle when a warm feeling comes over him. That same feeling that he got from Stephen when he was around. Jonathan gets up and looks around his room. The closer he walks to his window, the stronger that warm feeling gets. Now, standing at his window, he looks outside to see an older man waving at him. No, not waving at him, but trying to get his attention by frantically waving his arms. Jonathan initially gets spooked by this. He instantly recognizes the man as the homeless man from the park by school. Did he follow him home? Why is he trying so desperately to get Jonathan's attention? Jonathan just stares at the man as he continuously beckons him with his frantic arms. In any other situation, Jonathan would have just told his uncle and hid from the man. But that warm feeling, that instinctive feeling, is at its peak as he stares at the man. Without hesitation, Jonathan begins to walk out of his room to see what the man wants. Jonathan freezes as he is about to open his door. Remembering his fight with his uncle, Jonathan decides it's probably best to go out another way. Jonathan slides open his window and emerges into the outside world. Why is he going? This could be some creepy man or some serial killer trying to get their new victim. This all runs through his mind, but that feeling, that aura that he felt when around Stephen, is guiding him. This feeling makes him defy all logic and go out to talk with the homeless man.

As Jonathan gets closer to the man, reality hits him slowly. Jonathan begins to take smaller steps and eye the man cautiously.

"Come forward; don't stop," the man calls.

Jonathan hesitates, but that aura from before is stronger than ever. It is a warm feeling that is overtaking his body, almost as if some external force is trying to bring him to the strange man. Jonathan gets closer to the man but still keeps some distance between them. Now that he is closer, Jonathan begins to notice how strangely this man is dressed. The man is wearing a red and black vest with a long dress shirt underneath, black pants, and some really dirty black boots. He looks about in his mid-thirties, but his full head of gray hair makes him look older. His gray hair is greasy as if it hasn't been washed in weeks.

"Who are you?" Jonathan says.

"My name is Joseph Skrinner, but you can call me just Skrinner," the man says as he bows.

"What do you want from me? How long have you been outside my house?"

"That's it?"

"What do you mean?"

"I've been following you for days, Jonathan. You must pay better attention to your surroundings."

"Who the hell are you?!" he says, taking a few steps back.

"I'm not some random homeless man following you, although that is how I may appear. I must say I have not had a good chance to shower in quite some time. I came here and was looking for you, but when I found you, I decided to wait until I was sure it was you."

"What do you want from me?"

"In simple words? I was sent to this realm to find and bring you to my realm."

"Realm? What do you mean?"

"I am not from here; I am from another world. One similar to this one but far more natural. A friend of mine, a very powerful and insightful friend, sent me here to find you and bring you to my realm."

"Why do you keep saying realm?"

"Realm as in magical realm."

"Magic, like from the old world?"

"Yes. Now cut the crap—you know why I am coming to you."

"No, I don't. How do you know about the realms?"

"Because I am from the Red Realm, and I've come to take you there."

"That's not true; that's impossible."

"Look at me, kid. It is very possible."

"You're just fooling with me. Did someone from school set you up for this?"

"What? No. Kid, I am very short on time… can we cut this out? You know where I'm from, even if your logic doesn't let you believe it. I know deep down that you believe me."

Jonathan stares quietly at the oddly dressed man. As much as logic denies it, he has a point. The warm aura he was feeling earlier is radiating from this man.

"What do you need me for?"

"I am not entirely sure. A very powerful friend of

mine sent me here for you.”

“Why? What’s so special about me?”

“You are friends with Stephen, aren’t you?”

“How do you know that name?”

“Well, I’ve met him. He actually went with me to the Red Realm not so long ago.”

“Wait, he went with you?”

“Yes.”

“Everyone here thinks he’s dead, but not me.”

“Why didn’t you think that?”

Jonathan ponders that question. All logic pointed to Stephen being dead. Everyone told Jonathan that Stephen had run away from home and died. But Jonathan never believed it; he always had a feeling and instinct that Stephen wasn’t dead.

“I don’t know. I just had a feeling.”

Skrinner lets out a small smirk and then nods his head.

“A sort of warm aura, right? Usually around objects that were his, or in certain situations, this warm feeling materializes, almost as if something supernatural is trying to talk to you.”

“I’ve felt it for as long as I can remember, but you just described it perfectly,” Jonathan says, surprised.

“I described it perfectly because I also feel that same aura. Except we call it magic.”

“Magic, like from the old world?”

“Exactly like that.”

Jonathan stands there, absolutely bewildered. Not only did he just meet someone from the Red Realm, which he has read about since he was a young boy, but he is now being told that magic still exists and that some of that magic is with him.

"Why did Stephen leave with you?"

"Well, as you know, he did not have the best situation at home. One day, while I was visiting here, I found him crying in the park. We spoke, and I asked him to come with me."

"He chose to leave?"

"Yes, he basically said there was no reason to stay in this world except his friendship with you."

"You kidnapped him?"

"No. He voluntarily chose to leave; that is not kidnapping."

"If he went with you happily, then why are you here for me?"

"You don't belong here."

"What? What do you mean?" Jonathan asks.

"You know you don't. You have felt it throughout your entire life, that warm feeling, that aura that you feel. It's magic, not from this world but from mine. It's calling you; it's talking to you. You have magical potential, but this world is holding you back because it is drained of all magic. The magical potential in you is so strong, and in the Red Realm, it could truly flourish."

"How do you know all this?"

"Because I, too, have magical potential. I have done things with magic that would make some here consider me a god. You need to come with me."

"I'm not leaving. You're crazy."

"You don't believe anything I said?"

"No, I believe everything you said. Which is why I'm not going with you."

"That makes no sense."

"I have read about magic and the old world, and as

much as I want to be a part of it, I can't just leave my life here."

"Destiny is calling you, Jonathan, don't run from it. Chances like this don't come around often."

"I am not running away. Look, it was nice talking to you and getting real-life confirmation that magic is real and that I was right about Stephen, but I need to go back inside," Jonathan says as he begins walking back to his home.

"Wait!" Skrinner says, stepping forward.

"What is it?"

"I did come to recruit you, that is true. But the main reason I came to recruit you is because Stephen is missing."

"What do you mean?"

"Stephen was helping out at one of our satellite camps when it was raided. He and other rebellion soldiers were taken hostage. When he first joined me, he made me swear that if he was ever killed, I had to come and notify you."

"Is he missing? Or is he dead?"

"The Empire doesn't take many hostages for fun; most of the time they're tortured and then killed."

"So, the Red Realm Empire and insurgency are real?"

"Yes, most if not everything that you've read in the Book of Embers is true."

"Wait, did you come to tell me that I was right about him not being dead but also that he is dead?"

"Yes. But I am also stubborn like you. I do not think he is dead. I want to go on a rescue mission for him. I thought, 'What better way to rescue Stephen than by bringing you?'"

"I am not going with you; I already told you that."

"Then don't. Come with me and find Stephen; once you do, you can leave."

"Will he come back with me?"

"If he wants to, then yes, of course!"

Jonathan thinks about this proposal for a moment. He looks at the pleading old man and thinks about saving his friend. Jonathan then thinks about his aunt and uncle and how they would freak out if he was gone. But Jonathan knows that his life has not been the same without Stephen. With a deep breath, and not much thought put behind it, he says, "How long will I be gone?"

"Hopefully, not long. Time works differently in my realm. You could be gone for months but come back to find out that only a couple of minutes have passed."

Jonathan doesn't respond as he mulls over the decision.

"Do you trust me?"

"I shouldn't, but I do."

"Then come with me; save for your friend and bring him home."

"Fine, I'll go with you."

"Very well!" Skrinner says as he claps his hands together. He reaches into his red vest and pulls out a small red ball. Jonathan realizes that the vest is actually black, but it is just covered in red stains that look like blood. Skrinner plays with the small red ball in his hand. The red ball doesn't look entirely solid. It looks squishy, almost as if you squeezed the ball, it would erupt into liquid. The shell or skin of the ball is clear, and inside is a red liquid that fills about half of the ball.

"You know a lot about magic, don't you?"

"Yes, I mean some, but obviously not as much as you."

"I am glad you're a fan of my world. I am going to introduce you to a world full of pure magic, and it is beautiful. But hidden in that beauty, there are dangerous things and people. No matter what happens, you need to respond to me and trust me. Do you understand?"

This warning sends doubt into Jonathan's mind—now he begins to second guess his decision. But he doesn't let it deter him; he nods to show his approval.

"Good. This is an orb." Skrinner holds out the red orb to him and swishes it around. The red liquid moves around freely, and it almost shimmers. Jonathan can feel some magical aura radiating from the orb.

"This orb is going to take us to the Red Realm, which we call the Domum. These orbs are meant to transfer a couple of people between realms or across spaces in those realms. It is not the most efficient way to travel, but it works and allows even a low-level magician to open windows. Now beware, there are some symptoms that come with traveling by orb."

"Symptoms?"

"You will feel incredibly sick afterward or may even pass out depending on…"

"Pass out?"

"Don't worry, you should be fine."

Skrinner throws the red orb to the side, and it immediately evaporates. A small red portal opens up. The portal expands big enough that a couple of humans can walk through it and wide enough to fit a medium-sized car. The portal is a deep red, and the edges of it are pulsing, almost as if it is alive. Looking inside the portal, you see nothing but a sea of red.

Jonathan stares deeply into the red window as chills run down his spine. Seeing the pulsing portal sends doubt into his mind. None of this makes any logical sense. Yet somehow, it all makes sense to him because he's read about magic like this since he was young. Everything he has ever read about in his books of magic lay beyond the red portal. Yet his body is frozen, and his mind is racing. Beyond that red window lies a world of magic, monsters, and, most importantly, adventure.

Skrinner steps forward and is almost engulfed by the red window, but he stops. He turns back and notices the hesitation on Jonathan's face. Skrinner motions for Jonathan to step forward, but he doesn't. Jonathan stares deeply into the portal, almost as if entranced by it. His mind goes over every doubt and screams at him to not do this. Jonathan begins to open his mouth to tell Skrinner that he cannot go through with this. But before he can raise any concern, he feels his body being sucked up by the portal. His vision is now engulfed in red. His body is now moist as the red portal eats him. Jonathan feels like his head is spinning in all directions as he sees nothing but crimson red surrounding and licking him.

Skrinner jumps in shortly after and follows the tumbling Jonathan into the land of the unknown.

CHAPTER THREE

A blinding pulsing red light. A sea of red. The portal is moist and humid. Jonathan shoots out of the portal onto the brown soil which sticks to his wet skin. Gasping for breath, Jonathan is on the ground, fighting back vomit. His hands are covered in dirt. The red portal slowly starts to dim. A gust of wind hits him as the world comes into focus. Jonathan looks up to see that he is now in the middle of the woods. There is a thick layer of fog covering most of the trees. As Jonathan begins to stand up, he notices the fog covering the lower half of his body. There are so many trees, and all of them look identical. The fog is cold, yet there is a warm feeling associated with the ground. The trees tower above the fog and block out most of the sun. There is a slight scent of burning wood, but overall, this place feels oddly familiar to Jonathan.

"Are you okay?" Skrinner says as he helps Jonathan up.

"I feel like I'm spinning, but I almost threw up."

"Ah, first-timers," Skrinner says with a smirk.

"Where are we?" Jonathan asks, ignoring the slight.

Before Skrinner can respond, their conversation is silenced by a deafening howl. The howl echoes through the quiet trees and vibrates against every thick tree bark.

"Get down."

"What was that?" Jonathan says, as his voice cracks from fear.

"Get down!" Skrinner commands again.

Jonathan can tell by Skrinner's tone that the situation is serious. Jonathan runs up behind a tree and crouches. Skrinner does the same and takes a quick glance forward before making eye contact with Jonathan.

"I told you there is magic in this world, but there is also danger. Well, you are going to meet one of those dangers rather quickly; we are about to encounter a pack of werewolves."

"Werewolves?!"

Another cold howl pierces the misty forest. The sound of paws hitting the ground materializes as Skrinner moves from behind the tree into a small clearing. Jonathan watches in fear as Skrinner stands there, moving a finger to a nonexistent drum. Skrinner then draws two curved daggers from the back of his vest and forms a defensive stance. Jonathan's face goes cold. The sound of the paws and howls gets louder. Then, out of the fog, two black wolves launch themselves at Skrinner. Skrinner knocks the first wolf back with his dagger; as the wolf falls, it howls in anger. Skrinner then slashes the other wolf across the chest with his curved blade. The impact causes the wolf to hit the ground immediately, and it howls in pain. The dagger unveils red blood, and it stains the black fur of the beast. The first wolf howls, almost as if calling for help. Then, out of the mist, another wolf launches itself directly at Skrinner. Skrinner reacts quickly enough and brings both of his blades together to parry the wolf away. The parry cuts into the wolf's snout, and it retreats into the mist. Skrinner takes no time to return to his defensive stance. The trio of wolves disappear into the thick mist to regain their composure.

Skrinner does not break his stance or move. Suddenly, the three wolves howl and, in unison, launch themselves at Skrinner. One wolf jumps directly at Skrinner while the other two attack either side of him. The wolf that launches itself directly at Skrinner gets the majority of his attention. Skrinner times the distance perfectly and brings down the daggers as they slash across the face of the wolf and knock it down instantly. The other two wolves both crash into Skrinner and knock him down. The wolves snarl in excitement as they drag Skrinner into the mist.

"No!" Jonathan yells as he steps out of cover.

From the side, a force knocks Jonathan down. He feels the fur hit him as he slams into the ground. There was a fourth wolf stalking Jonathan, and when he moved from cover, it took the opportunity to strike. Jonathan scrambles to his feet, but the wolf charges at him. The wolf aims for Jonathan's neck and lurches forward with its sharp teeth. But Jonathan reacts promptly and kicks the wolf right in the snout. It snarls and retreats as Jonathan gets back on his feet. The wolf is now staring Jonathan down, trying to intimidate him. Jonathan notices the wolf is small and is covered in black fur. The wolf has piercing gray eyes. After pacing back and forth, the wolf growls as it launches itself at him. Jonathan reacts quickly enough and brings his arms forward to protect his face, but the force of the wolf knocks him off his feet. Jonathan lands against a tree that almost breaks his back. The wolf falls to the side but wastes no time and launches itself at Jonathan again.

This time, Jonathan isn't able to react quickly enough to fully defend his face. The wolf's teeth dig into the soft flesh of his arm as Jonathan screams. Jonathan tries to shake off the wolf, but it just bites down harder. Jonathan searches the ground for a rock or stick to defend himself with. The wolf bites down harder, and blood is now flowing out of the wound. Jonathan screams and tries pushing the wolf, but this just causes the wolf to clamp down even harder. Jonathan finds a sharp stone nearby, and he instantly slams it into the head of the wolf. This slightly dazes the wolf, but it still does not let go. Again, Jonathan smashes the stone into the head of the wolf, but this time harder. The wolf now lets go of Jonathan's arm and staggers backward. The wolf shakes its head a couple of times and then snarls at Jonathan. The wolf, now angrier than ever, launches itself again at Jonathan. Mistakenly, Jonathan brings up his injured arm to shield himself, and the wolf latches on again. At that point, the pain is so severe that Jonathan cannot scream, and with the force of the bite, Jonathan drops the stone. Jonathan begins frantically searching for another. As the teeth of the wolf dig deeper into his arm, Jonathan finds a smaller, sharper stone. He takes the sharp end of the stone and rams it into the wolf's head. The wolf snarls with the hit but bites down even harder. Jonathan yells in pain and anger and then jams the sharp end of the stone two more times into the head of the wolf. These hits cause immediate damage and the wolf releases. The wolf staggers backward, nearly falling off balance, blood oozing down the side of its head. Jonathan stands back up and stares at the dazed wolf swaying back and forth.

Again, the wolf snarls and launches itself again at him. With a precise blow, Jonathan drives the stone into the wolf's head in the same area as the previous hits. This hit sends the wolf flailing to the ground with a whimper. Jonathan stares down at the injured wolf, softly shaking on the ground. Blood is now covering the entire face of the wolf, continuously draining out of the wound. After a couple more movements, the wolf stops shaking and lays still. Jonathan is also shaking and breathing heavily as he is staring at the deceased animal. A mixture of horror and sadness settles in as the reality of the situation materializes.

"Jonathan, are you hurt?" Skrinner says as he jogs over. Jonathan was so preoccupied fighting that single wolf that he did not realize Skrinner somehow took care of the other remaining two. Skrinner is slightly nicked throughout his body, but other than that, he does not look too injured.

"My arm," Jonathan says as he lifts it to show Skrinner. His right forearm is deeply bruised from the teeth of the wolf, and it is steadily bleeding. Jonathan is in a mixture of shock and tears.

"Come here," Skrinner says as he cuts off one of his sleeves and ties it tightly around Jonathan's injured arm.

"When we get to base, you can get properly bandaged, but for now, that will do. Are you okay enough to continue?"

"I don't know. I know I am obviously hurt, but I don't really feel the pain all that much."

"That is adrenaline; trust me, you will feel it later. I am sorry you got hurt. I was trying to get to you as quickly as I could, but those other two had me beat for a while."

"It's not your fault; I think I handled myself okay," Jonathan says as he glances down at the wolf and its blood-stained face.

"You did that all by yourself?"

"Yes," Jonathan says coldly.

"You handled yourself pretty well. I must say, I am impressed."

"Impressed? Impressed by what?" Jonathan says defensively.

"You killed a werewolf all by yourself with no weapon and having only been in this realm for a few minutes. That is something to be proud of."

"I murdered a living thing; I am not proud to be a murderer."

"Murderer? Jonathan, if you did not kill that thing, it would have killed you with no mercy. You were protecting yourself."

Jonathan does not say anything in response. He is just standing there, shaking, and staring at the dead wolf, then back at his bloodstained hands.

"Jonathan, I know things work differently in your realm, but you need to understand this realm is dangerous, and there are dangerous creatures and people here. If you do not or choose not to defend yourself, you will be killed. I brought you here because I thought you were capable of handling yourself; however, I might have been wrong."

Again, Jonathan does not respond. He is just staring at the dead wolf that he killed… not with a weapon, but with his hands. Jonathan stares at his bloodstained hands and clothes; he is still shaking, and tears are still steadily flowing from his eyes.

"Jonathan, I can return you home if you'd wish, but if you choose to stay, I need you to be stronger."

Jonathan does not immediately respond. Instead, almost as if an unnatural force took over him, he says the unthinkable.

"I am not leaving until I find Stephen."

"Great! Now, let's get going. We need to get to the base as quickly as possible. The Misty Woods are dangerous, especially at night—the faster we get out of here, the better. Are you able to run?"

"I think so."

"Let us get going then." Skrinner marches forward.

Jonathan takes one last look at the dead body of the wolf and then chases after Skrinner.

The woods seem to stretch for miles, and the fog never seems to clear up, no matter how far they go. Surprisingly enough, they do not encounter any other living beings throughout the woods. Occasionally, a howl will cause them to run faster. Jonathan is slowly starting to stagger a bit behind; the injury is now becoming a bit more prevalent and is starting to really bother Jonathan. Eventually, Skrinner slows down when he notices that Jonathan has stopped running.

"Are you able to continue?"

"No, I don't think so. I need to rest."

"We can't stop, at least not here. A bit to the east, there is a small camp that might keep us safe for a bit. Think you can make it?"

"Yeah, I think so," Jonathan replies halfheartedly.

With that said, they continue running east. The howls seem to get louder the closer east they get.

After running for what seems like days, Skrinner slows down and hides behind a tree. Before Jonathan can speak, Skrinner motions for him to also take cover. For the most part, the area has all been the same, but now it is clear they are on elevated ground. Skrinner motions for Jonathan to stay quiet and then points at a group of hooded people.

The group is about 15 people, and they slowly march in unison through the woods. They are all wearing the same blue robe and are tugging along two horses and a wagon. There is a man in the center of the group who is hoodless and is chanting softly. The man is bald and has tattoos on the side of his head. The bald man is lightly humming something which the rest of the group repeats.

Skrinner then gets out from behind the tree and begins walking down to the group of people. By the manner Skrinner is approaching the group, Jonathan can gather that they must not be a threat.

"Ayt-e, it is a pleasure to see you and the People of Trent again," Skrinner says as he steps forward and bows his head to the tribe.

The bald man named Ayt-e steps forward through the ranks of his tribe and nods in return.

"My companion and I are seeking shelter from the lycans chasing us. Could you help us?"

"We do not want any trouble," the man says sternly.

"We do not mean to cause any trouble. I understand it is the time for your people's pilgrimage. However, we need your help."

Ayt-e is a stoic man who hardly even blinks and is firm with his responses. "We will not shelter you if it means coming into conflict with the wolves."

"We are with the rebellion and just need shelter momentarily, please. My companion is injured, and we cannot run any longer."

"We have no side in your war."

Jonathan pays little attention to Skrinner as he continues begging the group to shelter them. The sound of the howls is getting even closer. Jonathan is gripping his injured arm and starts to realize that there is a warm feeling radiating from something or someone from this group. Jonathan did not notice it initially due to the severe pain in his arm, but now that he's acknowledged it, he cannot seem to ignore it. The feeling or aura is similar to the one he felt around Stephen and similar to the one he felt when first approaching Skrinner. It has to be something related to magic. Jonathan notices that Ayt-e keeps glancing over at him while talking with Skrinner. Jonathan looks back and makes eye contact with the leader. Through an unspoken connection, Ayt-e realizes what is happening and nods.

"We will shelter you," Ayt-e says as he moves to the wagon and grabs an identical blue robe.

"We only have one extra robe. Skrinner, have your companion hide in the wagon amongst our gear."

"I don't think that is a good idea, Sire. He is wounded, and the wolves may smell his blood. We need to mask the smell of it by hiding him amongst your people."

"No. This robe will not fit him properly, and he will stand out to the Lycans. Do as I say, or we will not help you."

"Right, thank you. Your god, Altar, will honor your gratitude," Skrinner says as he slips on the robe.

"Lower the wagon," Ayt-e commands his people. The two people pulling the wagon stop and lower the wagon. Ayt-e walks over and removes the cover of the wagon. There are various items hidden under it: cooking pots, clothing, and some books.

"Get in between the items—whatever happens, do not move!" Skrinner commands as Jonathan jumps onto the wagon.

"What happens if they smell the blood?"

"They won't—we will cover for you. Now, get down."

Jonathan notices one of the People of Trent staring at him. Jonathan now pinpoints that the aura he initially felt is coming from that individual.

"Jonathan, get down now." Jonathan drops down as Skrinner and Ayt-e cover the wagon once again. The two tribespeople that were pulling the wagon pick it back up and slowly begin marching forward. Skrinner takes his place towards the middle of the group, right next to Ayt-e, who begins slowly chanting as the group marches forward.

Jonathan cannot make out what Ayt-e or the group is chanting, but it sounds haunting. As the group marches along, Jonathan feels the aura from the person who had been staring at him growing stronger.

As the group marches along, the sound of the oncoming pack of wolves gets louder and louder. The tribe does not seem to march faster. Instead, they keep at their slow and steady pace. Jonathan tries his best to remain calm as the pack of wolves finally catches up to the group.

Jonathan can hear the snarls and growls of the wolves as they arrive at the tribe. The People of Trent halt but do not turn to face the pack. They stopped in a small clearing in the towering trees; to the left, there was a big rock that could be mistaken for a hill because of the way it blends into the ground.

Skrinner does not directly look at the pack, but he can tell this pack is different from the one from before. These wolves stand on their hind legs and are much bigger than the others. These wolves are covered in silver fur and have blood-red eyes. Skrinner immediately determines that this is a pack of lycans and not werewolves like the previous group, making this pack much more dangerous. The pack of lycans separate and start circling the tribe in a clockwise motion. Jonathan holds his breath as he hears the Lycans panting in hunger. Skrinner takes note of four lycans circling them, but he also notices that one Lycan is standing on the stone and observing them all. Skrinner has a good idea of who it is, but he does not divert his attention to the leader so as to not attract attention. Eventually, the lead lycan jumps down from the stone and stands directly in front of the tribe.

The entire tribe is facing in the direction of the lead lycan but not looking at the lycan directly. This gives Skrinner a chance to examine the lycan better. The lycan stands out mainly because it is much bigger than the rest and has dark black fur. The wolf has a scar across its right eye that makes it look shut. The sunlight is piercing through the leaves of the towering trees, making the lycan's red eyes stand out more. The lycan is bigger than any wolf or human, and towers over the group. The lycan is wearing a metal chest plate from which a small knife dangles. It is clear that this lycan is the leader of the pack and is very different from the others they previously encountered. Skrinner has not met this creature before, but he has heard about him. Lykos is the leader of the lycans, werewolves, and Red Realm Empire. He is a brutal military general who shows no mercy to those who oppose the rule of the Empire.

"We are searching for two runaways: a man and a boy. They ran in this direction. Have you seen them?" Lykos speaks with a deep voice that could almost be mistaken for a growl.

Ayt-e steps forward, and the tribe parts so he can walk through.

"Lykos, it is an honor to see you once again. However, we have not encountered any runaways."

"You haven't seen them?" the lycan says while sniffing the air.

"No one has run this way, General."

Lykos steps up to Ayt-e and is now towering above him as he speaks. However, Ayt-e keeps his same stoic demeanor.

"I don't think you understand the severity of this situation. I am searching for two criminals of the Empire. Any attempt to hide them will be seen as an act of treason, thereby making you all criminals."

"I repeat myself, Sire; we have not seen them."

Lykos turns his head and snarls loudly, now getting directly in Ayt-e's face.

"Lies! We have traced their foul smell to your group. If they hide amongst your group, you and your people will pay a price so severe that not even your god could save you."

"The People of Trent have no bidding in your war and only wish to continue our pilgrimage."

"Search them and their belongings!" Lykos commands. The other three lycans then stand on their hind legs and begin ransacking the people. Even on their hind legs, these other lycans are nowhere near as tall as their leader.

One of the lycans grabs a woman by the shoulder, gripping her softly so as not to pierce her flesh with its sharp claws. She squirms slightly in obvious fear of the creature. This frustrates the lycan, and he throws her to the side. The power of the beast is shown by how easily it throws the woman. The woman hits the ground hard, and all her belongings fall out of her bag as her hood falls off.

Skrinner has to try his best to keep his poise and not break his blank stare. Another lycan grabs at a younger girl and snatches a brown satchel from under her robe. The lycan rummages through the bag, pulling out various items, but then stops when it pulls out a charm. The lycan eyes a gold necklace with a big green jewel. After some moments of observing the charm, the lycan tosses it aside. The lead lycan, Lykos, walks towards the charm on the ground and picks it up, admiring the green jewel.

Jonathan is trying his best to keep as still as possible even though there is plenty of chaos going on around him. He could hear the charm hit the ground, and that was when it clicked for him. The aura that he felt wasn't from the woman; it was from that charm. Now that the charm is out, he realizes the energy he felt is coming from that necklace. There is something unusual about it; the magic radiating from it is different from the one he felt from Stephen and Skrinner. It radiates some energy that he cannot explain, but somehow, he feels drawn to it.

"Sire. Please, return that to her," Ayt-e commands.

Lykos lets out a small smile as he realizes he now has the upper hand.

"Not till the two criminals reveal themselves."

"I have already told you we have not seen them."

Lykos walks forward, cutting through the first row of the tribe, and is now standing right in front of Ayt-e, who remains still. Ayt-e does not waiver in front of the massive creature in front of him. Nothing seems to disrupt the peace within Ayt-e.

Lykos reaches forward, pulls Ayt-e by the robe, and throws him to the ground. Ayt-e hits the ground hard, but again, does not seem to give in or fight back. In this action,

Lykos lets go of the charm, and the young girl rushes for the necklace. Lykos steps down on the girl's hand and pins it to the ground. She yells in retort as Lykos lets out a small smirk. Lykos picks her up by her arm and throws her to the side. The girl crashes into the ground headfirst and immediately stops moving. Lykos then signals for his underling to bring the necklace to him, which he does. Lykos holds the gold necklace and observes it closely, trying to figure out what is so special about this necklace.

Jonathan is panicking under the tarp. He cannot see what is going on, but it sounds like the pack of lycans will eventually catch him. Skrinner has now broken his stare and is eyeing the crazed lycan observing the necklace. Skrinner has also felt the magic from the charm; not as much as Jonathan, but nonetheless, it is obvious to any being of magic that the necklace is infused with magic.

"This necklace would be worth nothing; why does she care so much for it?"

"That is her mother, Mara's, charm," Ayt-e responds as he stands back up.

As Lykos holds up the necklace, Jonathan can feel the necklace vibrating as if it is calling him. The vibrations from the charm are almost singing softly to him.

Instantly, one of the hooded people charges at Lykos in anger. Lykos throws his free hand forward, and it stabs into the man's chest as he screams. Lykos' claw penetrates so deep that it emerges from the man's back. Lykos shakes the body of the man and then removes his claw as the man slumps dead to the ground.

"Now I've had enough of this banter. The runaways must reveal themselves now, or you will all be killed."

Skrinner stares at the dead man, with the necklace now

also humming furiously to him. Something comes over him, and Skrinner does the unimaginable; he steps forward.

MARIO A HERNANDEZ

Chapter Four

Skrinner steps forward, and the group goes silent. Lykos stares him down as Skrinner removes the robe. As the robe falls, Skrinner unveils his two curved daggers from the back of his vest.

"Ah, there he is. I knew you would not stand by much longer as these innocent people suffered," Lykos says.

"I see the Empire has not given up hurting civilians."

Lykos snarls loudly, and this signals the other lycans to charge at Skrinner. As the lycans begin to charge at Skrinner, someone jumps from atop the hill and slashes their sword across the back of one of the lycans. The lycan howls into the air, but before it can acknowledge the attacker, they stab the sword cleanly into the chest of the beast, killing it instantly. The other lycan charges at the man, who quickly stabs the lycan and pushes him away. Lykos is about to charge forward at the attacker, but the attacker is prepared and slices the wind with his sword. If Lykos had charged forward, the sword would have caused major damage to him. Lykos stops in his tracks and growls at the attacker. Without breaking eye contact with the creature, the attacker says, "Run!"

Skrinner runs to the wagon and uncovers it to reveal a shaken Jonathan. "Let's go!"

Jonathan jumps out of the wagon. Once Jonathan is out of the wagon, the People of Trent begin marching in the opposite direction. However, they do not run. Skrinner nods at Jonathan, who begins running. Just before Jonathan takes off, he picks up the charm and runs. As they run, they can hear the sound of a sword hitting metal, followed by a howl.

Jonathan and Skrinner run until they come upon another clearing. To the left are a small group of rocks huddled together. Jonathan takes note of the unusual setup of rocks as Skrinner walks towards them.

"How's your arm?"

"It hurts, but I guess running into the werewolves got my mind off it."

"Lycans actually."

"What?"

"The beasts that we just encountered are lycans; the other beasts we encountered first are werewolves."

"There's a difference?"

"Yes, a big one."

"What are the differences?"

"I will tell you shortly. Help me move this stone," Skrinner says as he bends to push one of the larger rocks from the group. Together, they push the rock forward, and to Jonathan's surprise, it slides smoothly across the ground. Once the rock is moved, Jonathan notices it is masking a trap door. After struggling for some time, Skrinner gets the door to open. The door leads to darkness.

"This is a safe house; it hasn't been used in some time, but it can provide us some shelter. Climb down first."

Jonathan just stares down at the darkness.

"It is perfectly safe—there is a ladder against the door… just feel for it and climb down."

"I can't see anything… how am I supposed to find the ladder?"

"Just reach for it; it cannot be that far."

Before Jonathan has a chance to respond, someone comes running out of the trees into the clearing. Skrinner steps forward and draws his two curved daggers. As quickly as Skrinner draws the weapons, he puts them back—it is the man who saved them earlier. The man is tall and has long black hair with a sword holstered on his back. He has sharp green eyes and light brown skin caked in dirt. He is also wearing a metal back and chest plate, the front of which has a large X painted on it in what seems to be blood. Underneath, he is wearing a dark gray uniform.

"Dango, I have never been so excited to see you," Skrinner says as he walks forward to hug the man. For the first time, the always-serious man named Dango lets out a big smile and hugs Skrinner.

"You're lucky I was on my way to my den, or else Lykos would have killed you both," Dango says with a small nod toward Jonathan.

"Dango, this is Jonathan."

"Pleasure to meet you, Jonathan. Don't let this old man scare you; this realm isn't as dangerous as he makes it out to be. It's just most people want your Skrinner dead!" Dango says with a laugh. Jonathan and Dango shake hands very awkwardly.

"We should get inside. I did not kill Lykos, but I stalled him long enough to get away."

They return to the hidden door, which is pretty much

invisible unless you know it's there. Dango pulls open the door, much faster than Skrinner did, to reveal the dark hole. Dango squats near the entrance and points.

"That is the ladder; hard to see and probably older than Skrinner, but it will hold."

Hanging from the trapdoor is a rope ladder that heads down into the never-ending darkness. Jonathan turns to Skrinner, who just motions to the ladder. Jonathan is the first to climb down the ladder into a dark cave. As soon as he gets into the darkness of the cave, the humidity from within strikes him. Jonathan is followed then by Skrinner and Dango, who closes the door and officially encloses them in complete darkness.

I can't see the next step!" Jonathan yells as he slightly panics in the humid darkness.

"Just keep going, you're almost there," Dango encourages.

Jonathan sucks in his fears and continues the downward trek into the darkness. To his surprise, after a couple more seconds of climbing, he eventually felt the ground again.

"I think I hit the surface."

"Good, step off and step back so we can come down without hurting you," Dango commands. Jonathan steps onto the ground again and takes a few steps back into the darkness. However, he does not go too far back as he does not know what lies in the darkness. Shortly after his arrival, Skrinner and then Dango come down from the ladder. As he finishes coming down, Dango turns to Skrinner.

"Saved you there, didn't I?" Dango's voice is broad and powerful.

Skrinner waves his hand as if it was no big deal.

"How much food do you have?"

"Uh, I have not restocked recently, but there should be enough to last us about two days."

"What happened to all the stock you've put into this dump?"

"You aren't my only visitors, you know?"

"We have to stay here as long as possible; we don't know how long our scent will linger above."

"That's why I brought us here, Master. Have you forgotten about the scent tracing we have done to this place?"

"Ah, you're right. Then maybe just eat, rest, and make way first thing in the morning."

"I'm glad you remember; you've slowly become more forgetful in your old age!" Dango says as he lights a candle.

"I am not that much older than you, and anyways, you've become more and more like a tamwah."

Dango stares down at his nonexistent stomach, then back up at Skrinner. Dango and Skrinner stare at each other, and then they burst out laughing.

"It is good to see you, Dango," Skrinner says with a smile.

"I am glad to see you again, Master," the man named Dango says.

"You both can take a seat. I'll warm up a pot of Cof," Dango says as he walks toward a cabinet and pulls out a small rusty kettle. He then pours some brown powder into it and fills the kettle with water from a nearby bucket. He then lights a fire and puts the kettle over it. Instantly, the smell of coffee fills the air and surrounds the cave.

Meanwhile, Jonathan is exploring the cave with his eyes. The cave isn't that big; at most, six people could fit in here. There are various items stored across the cave: cooking items, weapons, and some food items. The walls of the cave are marked with some paint. The more Jonathan pays attention to the walls, the more he realizes they are wall paintings and not just random paint marks. The paintings remind him of the ancient cave paintings he learned about in history. The paintings are really old and are hard to make out, but he feels drawn to them.

"Interested in art?" Skrinner asks.

"They're paintings from a long time ago; they depict the story of the first Myronids," Dango responds.

"The who?"

"The Myronids used to be the protectors of the Red Realm. They were warriors and magicians, and they helped fight against those who practiced dark magic, the Mangalum."

"Dark magic? Like black magic?" Jonathan asks.

"Yes," Dango responds firmly.

Jonathan then turns his attention to Skrinner, who is now also staring at the paintings.

"You were telling me about the lycans and werewolves—could you tell me more?"

"Werewolves are generally smaller and more wolf-like. They were blooded when there was not a full moon, therefore they are not considered full-blooded. Lycans are more human-like and are generally bigger and stronger. They were blooded during a full moon by another lycan," Skrinner mentions.

"That's actually really fascinating. The Book of Embers only mentions werewolves."

"That book was written way before they were prevalent."

Dango walks to the table and drops off three silver

cups with Cof. Skrinner takes a long slow sip of his drink, while Jonathan just holds the warm cup. Dango periodically takes small sips of his drink.

"You have been gone for a long time, Skrinner; things have changed."

"I know, I got caught up in my pursuit of our changeling."

"Do you know where Stephen is?" Jonathan buts in.

"You know Stephen?" Dango responds.

"Of course, I know him. He's my best friend. That's why I'm here; I'm going to bring him back."

"Bring him back?" Dango says with a stir.

"I'm going to bring him back home."

"And where is home?" Skrinner says with a pondering eye.

"Earth," Jonathan says half-heartedly, still unsure of where exactly he is. "Is this still Earth?"

Dango and Skrinner look at each other as if non-verbally deciding who is going to speak. Although not said, it is obvious that these two share a history together.

Dango leans forward in his chair. "We are in the Red Realm. It is part of the five realms which make up the universe. Your planet, Earth, is part of the five realms. It is actually the Yellow Realm. So, in total there are five; Red, Blue, Green, Yellow, and Purple. Long ago, the five realms were united by an interdimensional bridge that allowed people from all realms to travel to other realms freely. This led the realms to unite and create the Five Realm Council, which ruled over the realms with one goal in mind; to provide the best life for those in the five realms."

"Wait, so the Earth is connected here?"

"No, not anymore; the bridge was last active centuries

ago. Eventually, a group of anarchists started a war between the realms, and in turn, the bridge was destroyed by the mages of the time."

"For knowing so much about our world, you sure don't know that much," Skrinner teases.

"Leave the boy alone, Skrinner. I don't think the Book of Embers talks about the history of the realm," Dango says, defending Jonathan.

"Anyways, after the bridge was destroyed, each realm was basically left on its own. Magic flourished in some realms like the Purple Realm but died in others like the Yellow Realm. The Green, Blue, and Red Realms still hold magic, but not as much as they used to. When the bridge was destroyed, the Red Realm became a republic. Unfortunately, this did not last as corruption and greed took over, and the Republic eventually was taken over by extremists. Many of the members of the Anarchy of Powers, who destroyed the bridge, infiltrated the councils and created the Red Realm Empire, which still stands today."

"And you both are enemies of the Empire?"

"Technically, yes, but we prefer to be called insurgents or rebels," Dango laughs.

"Stephen came here to fight the Empire?"

"He came here to live the life you and he always dreamed of. A life of magic and adventure. I was hesitant to bring him here, but after some time, I realized he was destined for a bit more than we ever thought."

"What do you mean?"

"Stephen might have only just left you in your realm, but he has been here for some time and has changed a bit. Stephen is a great person, but more importantly, he is a great and noble warrior. Which is part of the reason why

Rite chose to train him as his successor."

"Warrior? What did he fight? Who's Rite?"

"The ruling council of the Empire has four members, and only one is a former councilman, Nes. Nes represents us and our cause. Our hope is to restore the Red Realm to a republic, the way it was during the times of the Five Realm Council. When the Five Realm Council was at its peak, it had a grand army and special military leaders known as the Myronids. The Myronids are users of light magic; they protected the Republic and everything it stood for. When the Empire took over, they created the Mangalum, who were users of dark magic. Together, they destroyed everything the Republic built and wiped out almost all of the Myronids, as they were the biggest threat to their power. The last surviving Myronid is Rite; he is also part of our insurgency. He has been looking for new members to create a new order of Myronids. Rite believes that in order to truly defeat the Empire, we will need Myronids. When Rite and Stephen first met, Rite insisted that Stephen be trained.

"The magical potential in you is also something he shared. Every aura and feeling you have ever felt has come from the magical potential inside you."

"What happened to him?"

Dango shoots Skrinner a quick glance. "He's off somewhere, training with Rite. Rite is the last living Myronid. The training of a Myronid takes years."

"So, how will I find him? How will we get back?"

"I can take you back, I just need to find another orb. However, we heard about Rite and Stephen being ambushed by the Empire. Rite came back to us and told us that they either took or killed Stephen."

"You're telling me he could be dead?!"

"Lower your voice, we are still hiding," Skrinner says sharply.

"Why am I here?"

"You came here to find Stephen."

"No, no, you brought me here; you convinced me. Why me?"

"When I went looking for Stephen, I was drawn to you. You have strong magical potential; I have never felt anything like it before. Your world is so devoid of all magic that you and Stephen stood out like a sore thumb to any magical being."

"What are you trying to say?"

"It has been a pattern since the existence of this realm that every millennium, two mages are born: one destined to be the Prophet of Light Magic and the other for Dark Magic. I believe you are the Prophet of Light Magic."

"I don't understand."

"I think you are the Prophet, the one who is destined to destroy the Red Realm Empire and destroy the Manga-lum, but most importantly, I think you are the one who will restore the Republic."

Chapter Five

What? No, you must be mistaken. I am not your Prophet. I barely even knew magic really existed up until a few hours ago. Now you're telling me I am the savior of this world."

"Magic has no direction. I am sure you were chosen for a reason. The potential in you is unmistakable."

"What am I supposed to do? Get a sword and take on the entire Empire?"

"Magic isn't that simple. I am not sure of the entire workings of the mages. That is something you will have to talk with Magiya about."

"Who is that?"

"Magiya is probably the eldest mage in existence. Magiya was the mage born in the previous millennium and has been an ally of the Rebellion from the start."

"And he can tell if I'm the Prophet or not?"

"Yes," Skrinner replies quickly.

"What if I'm not?"

"Then, after we find Stephen, I will take you back home."

"You have to swear to me that you will, even if we

don't find Stephen."

"I swear." Skrinner crosses his heart and then takes another big sip from his drink.

"You know, I'm having a hard time believing you."

"Skrinner is many things, but he is not a liar," Dango interjects as he stands up.

"Anyway, we should get some rest—we have a big journey tomorrow back to base. Find a spot you like and get comfortable. If you need to get rid of any waste, just take a candle and head further into the cave. There are no other living beings in this cave, so you can use it in peace," Dango says as he lies down by the last step of the ladder.

Jonathan positions himself across from Skrinner, who is on the other side of the table. Skrinner just lays down and seemingly falls asleep right away. Jonathan struggles a bit to get comfortable on the somehow moist ground. After some turns, Jonathan finds a position that is serviceable enough and tries to close his eyes. Jonathan ponders if, once he closes his eyes, he will wake up back home, laughing and realizing this was all just some vivid fever dream. No matter how much he tells himself that possibility, he knows deep down that this is not a dream—this is reality. At least his dreams will not be filled with werewolves or lycans.

Jonathan wakes up to pure darkness and humidity. He jumps up from the ground and tries to figure out where he is. For a moment, he contemplates if he is dead. But then he crashes into the table in the center of the cave. The sound wakes up Dango and Skrinner, who jump up, ready to fight. After noticing it was just Jonathan, Dango relights the candle, and they slowly start to wake up. The trio do not say a word to each other. Dango retreats to brew another pot of Cof, while Skrinner and Jonathan sit at the table. They are all obviously still groggy from sleep.

"I will not miss sleeping here," Dango exclaims.

"What happened to the cots that we had here?"

"I moved them back to base. We don't really use this hideout anymore, and if we do, it is only for a couple of hours."

After some time, Dango comes by to drop off cups of Cof and some odd-looking food. Jonathan is just staring at the strange food.

"What is this?" Jonathan asks as politely as possible.

"It is a Gelatious plant. It is really healthy for you—try it," Skrinner responds.

Jonathan continues eyeing the green stem. The plant is hard and stiff. Without much thought, Jonathan picks it up and bites into it. The bite is accompanied by a large crunching sound. The plant has a bitter taste, almost similar to that of kale.

"I'm guessing you aren't a fan of it," Skrinner mentions.

"I don't like many vegetables, but I need food." Jonathan winces as he takes another crunch of the plant.

After eating and sitting for quite some time, the trio are disturbed by a loud sound from above. The trio immediately freeze when they hear the sound. The sound strikes again, but this time louder. The sound comes from above, from the area of the trap door. The trio are now standing, and Dango rushes over to put his holster back on and draws his sword.

Skrinner draws his two curved daggers from his blood-red vest. "I have a feeling we were just found," Skrinner mentions.

"What is the plan? We are not close enough to base to make it before they find us," Dango adds.

"We have to try. Jonathan, you need to head out first. We can provide you with protection. We need you to keep running until you hit a lake. When you get there, find shelter and wait for us. We will come to you."

Jonathan nods in approval. Dango walks over to one of the many piles of weapons and grabs a couple. Dango motions Jonathan over, then begins showing him the weapons: a metal war hammer, a mace, and a sword in a black holster. Jonathan feels some magic radiating from the sword. Before Dango can even ask, Jonathan mentions, "I want the sword."

Dango looks shocked by the apparent initiative that Jonathan shows. He then tosses the weapon to Jonathan. As soon as Jonathan catches it, the connection is established. The holster is made of a fine leather material, and the handle of the sword stands out from the holster. Jonathan draws the sword. It is a simple gold hilt with a smooth black layer of leather covering it and a snake sketched into the leather. The pommel is a vibrant gold color. The sword is heavy, but it feels light in his hands. "Wait, is that…"

"Yes, it is. I hope you don't mind," Dango interrupts Skrinner.

"What's wrong with the sword?" Jonathan asks.

"Absolutely nothing; it belongs to an old friend of mine," Skrinner mentions.

"Test it out," Dango encourages.

Jonathan draws the sword and swings it around. The handle of the weapon fits perfectly in his hands, and it moves so freely yet in complete control in his hands.

"I like it; it almost feels like it was made for me. But

what is this hole here for?" In the pommel of the sword, there is an opening, as if something used to be there.

"That is for a crystal. That sword used to belong to Marvius; he was a Myronid. Every Myronid sword has a crystal in it. It links with the user and grants them some enhanced abilities depending on the color of the stone. When the user dies, the crystal does as well," Skrinner informs Jonathan, who stares at the blade, now realizing why it was attracting him.

"Jonathan, you need to run towards the opening of the cave. Run till you find the lake. And if you need to, use the sword. Use it carefully; we will catch up with you shortly." Skrinner informs Jonathan of the plan as the sounds from above get louder. In an instant, the trap door from above gets blown up, and the sunlight from above invades the darkness of the cave. A werewolf comes diving down the cave. Dango reacts promptly and slices the werewolf's neck as soon as it lands.

"Jonathan, go now!" Skrinner yells as he takes a defensive stance.

Jonathan takes off running to the mouth of the cave. As Jonathan is fleeing, he can hear howls coming from the main part of the cave. The width and height of the cave get smaller and tighter as he progresses through the cave. The air also seems to get thinner as the ground gets more and more moist. In the main part of the cave, the ground was rough dry dirt. But now the ground is becoming moist as he seemingly gets closer to the lake. After some moments of peril, he finally starts to see a piercing light shining from the mouth of the tunnel. The opening of the cave is smaller than the actual tunnel; it isn't very wide either. One average-sized person could barely fit through the tunnel. Jonathan runs out of the cave into the cold air outside. Jonathan emerges onto a small patch of dirt that slowly leads to the lake. This area looks devoid of the towering trees from the Misty Woods. Jonathan takes peace in the quiet area. The water from the lake is calm. The lake is surrounded by two patches of land and the cave which is directly in front of it. Jonathan searches the area with his eyes for any potential enemies or threats. Once he sees that the coast is clear, he relaxes and takes in a breath of fresh air. Jonathan then sets up behind a smaller tree and waits for his companions.

Jonathan begins looking around the land. The water is crystal clear, and there doesn't seem to be any fish. The area around the lake looks empty as well. Jonathan begins wondering just how big this land is. He has seemingly explored so much of it, while also not really exploring anything. With some downtime, he begins pondering what Skrinner told him. Skrinner called him the Prophet. He is supposed to lead the Rebellion to victory over the Red Realm Empire. How could he possibly be the savior of these people? How could he be a hero to a group of people he just met? Is this all a dream or some sort of twisted illusion? Or is he really destined to be a savior?

Jonathan's train of thought is broken up as he gets tackled to the ground from behind. Jonathan wrestles back against a hairy opponent. A werewolf is on top of Jonathan; he can feel the fur and force of the creature as it tries to bite him. As he fell from being tackled, the sword flew from his hand and landed several feet away from him. Jonathan squirms under the grip of the wolf, and the creature digs its claws into Jonathan's arms and pins him to the ground. Jonathan is staring directly into the face of the hellish creature. It has bright yellow eyes and a mouth full of many jagged sharp teeth; it is almost drooling with hunger as it snarls at Jonathan. Again, Jonathan squirms under the grip of the werewolf, but this causes the wolf to dig its claws deeper into the soft flesh of Jonathan's arms. As the claws go deeper into his flesh, Jonathan yells out in pain. The wolf seems to let out a small smile as Jonathan yells.

With a gush of wind, a small knife flies through the air and digs itself into the neck of the werewolf. In the rush of the moment, the werewolf turns to the direction that the knife came from and howls loudly at its attacker. Jonathan turns to see the assailant as well; he sees a man with a long black trench coat and short, slick blonde hair. The man throws another knife at the wolf. The knife sails through the air, almost as if whistling off the wind, and stabs into the front of the wolf's neck. A small gurgling sound comes from the wolf, and then it falls backward, dead.

Jonathan gets up and runs to his sword. He grabs it and draws the sword as he faces the knife-wielding assailant. The man stops in place and slowly raises both of his hands.

"I do not wish to harm you," the man says with a soft voice.

"Who are you?" Jonathan asks, the sword still raised.

"I think the question is, who are you? Are you friendly? Or do I have to put a knife through your neck too?"

"I am with Mr. Skrinner and Dango," Jonathan responds.

"Ha! He prefers Skrinner; he says the 'Mr.' makes him old. Can you believe that old man?" The man says as he walks forward and wipes his hands on his trench coat. The trench coat is tattered and torn in places, and the man is wearing fingerless gloves that reveal his dirty fingers. The man is now standing in striking distance, but Jonathan doesn't attack him.

"My name is Nox, and it is a pleasure to meet you." The man extends his hand and bows.

"Jonathan," he says as they shake hands. Jonathan notices that Nox has green eyes and several bandoliers under his trench coat with hundreds of small throwing knives attached to it.

Nox walks to the carcass of the werewolf and retrieves his knives, which he then cleans on the ground. Nox then returns them to the empty spots on the many bandoliers that he has hidden under his coat.

"Where are Skrinner and Dango?"

"They are inside the cave; we were attacked."

"Ah, okay. Well, come on," Nox says as he turns to the lake.

"What do you mean?"

"We have to leave; there's no guarantee that they survived. I assume you are the person that Skrinner brought from the Yellow Realm, which means I need to get you to the camp."

"I'm not going with you."

"Why not?" Nox says as he turns to Jonathan.

"I was told to wait here, and I don't really know who you are. Why should I trust you?"

"Trust me, kid. If I wanted to kill you, I would've done so already."

"That doesn't fill me with confidence…"

"If Skrinner and Dango were killed, what would you do?"

"I don't know."

"Exactly. I was summoned to help escort you to the camp."

"Summoned by who?"

"I will explain everything when we reach the camp. Come on, I can't risk the attackers finding me here. I am not much of a fighter like Skrinner and Dango."

"No. You need to tell me now," Jonathan says as he raises the sword.

Nox walks towards Jonathan, who is holding up the sword defensively. Although the sword is held up sternly, Nox can sense the uncertainty behind it. Nox reaches for the sword, but Jonathan responds by stabbing forward. Nox swipes the sword downwards and throws a punch at him. The punch is fast, but he delivers it with precision; it knocks Jonathan back. Nox advances, sweeps Jonathan's leg, and knocks him flat on his back. Jonathan grunts as he hits the dirt. Nox stands over him.

"Are you done? As I mentioned, I cannot fight off a wave of werewolves. I am a diplomat with a knife, not a warrior." Jonathan ignores Nox.

Nox extends his hand to the fallen Jonathan.

"Magiya called for me. The camp that I am referring to is one of the bases for the Rebellion; you will be safe there."

After seconds of hesitation, Jonathan gives in and stands up. He retrieves the sword and places it back in the holster. He then slings the holster over his shoulder.

"Sorry."

"No need to apologize. Your skills are there, but they're untrained. With a bit of help, you can be a fine warrior." Their conversation is cut short as Dango and Skrinner emerge from the mouth of the cave. They both have small cuts and bruises, but other than that, they look unharmed.

"I see you found a friend," Skrinner says.

"Hardly," Nox says with a shrug.

They all shake hands with Nox and have a short conversation about the attackers. Jonathan is in on the conversation at first, but then he tunes out as he gets lost in all this talk about rebellions and empires. After a couple of minutes of conversing, the group began walking around the perimeter of the lake. The plan is to walk on the outskirts of the lake to reach the camp. Skrinner and Dango lead the group, while Nox and Jonathan follow. Dango and Skrinner are talking amongst themselves the entire time. Nox and Jonathan march along quietly until Nox breaks the silence between the two.

"So, how do you like it here so far?"

"It's pretty crazy here. Every moment of peace is ruined by some attack. But I think it's also really nice here."

"That is a good understanding of this realm. Did you come here to be a soldier?"

"No, not really. I came here looking for my friend Stephen."

"Stephen. Yes, as far as I remember, he is training with Rite."

"Yeah, they told me. Which means I basically came here for no reason."

"How long have you been here?"

"I don't know. I just got here before the attack in the cave."

"That's interesting. What is your plan to find Stephen?"

"I don't know. But Skrinner said he could take me back home after. So, in the meantime, I am just here."

"Just a small tip; despite the craziness of the realm,

it is really quite beautiful here. You need to learn to take joy in small and quiet moments like these. This realm is so beautiful and holds so many wonders; unfortunately, the constant wars have robbed the world of its natural beauty."

"How long have they been going on?"

"As long as I can remember. Frankly, I am not much of a soldier. When I was young, my family pushed me towards a life as a politician. I actually served on the Five Realm Council at one point. Wait, do you know what that is?"

"Yes, they told me. What made you stop?"

"Well, it was destroyed. Then the real fighting began. People joined sides, and I joined the freedom fighters here."

"You seem tired," Jonathan says sternly.

"I am a realist, Jonathan. This war has been going on for far too long. Many have died, yet nothing has really changed. I am one of the only people who just want the war to end. Take this from someone who served in the Republic before and has closely observed the Empire; nothing significant has changed under any regime, just who is responsible for the lack of changes."

After that, Nox falls silent. Skrinner and Dango still talk amongst themselves. Jonathan tunes in and out of their conversation but never truly pays attention to it. However, Jonathan begins to notice how he has yet to feel hungry or tired and has seemingly forgotten about his wounded arm. Jonathan has surely been here for at least a couple of hours; maybe because of the time difference? Jonathan is taken out of the thought by a yell. Snapping back to reality, he pins the yell to Skrinner. A couple of yards behind the group are a duo of what look like people with pointy ears. They have white pasty skin with pointy ears and a sharp pointy face. They have light armor on their shoulders and chest. They are carrying a bow and arrows. Jonathan turns to see the assailants and immediately recognizes that they are goblins. The goblins load their bows and take aim at them.

"Into the lake!" Skrinner yells. Without hesitation, Dango and Skrinner dive into the lake. Nox waits for Jonathan, but he hesitates.

"Can you swim?" Nox says frantically.

"Yes, I just don't know what I will do with an injured arm."

"We will help you if needed, but we need to go now."

Jonathan responds with a small nod. Then Nox plunges into the lake. Again, Jonathan hesitates, and in that quick moment of hesitation, an arrow digs itself into his right thigh. Jonathan yells as the tip of the arrow digs into the soft flesh. Jonathan drops to one knee in pain. This move causes the other arrow that was shot at him to fly over his head. Jonathan takes a deep breath, jumps up, and dives headfirst into the lake.

Jonathan lets out a cry of pain as the cold water hits the wound, but the cry is stopped short as the cold water engulfs him. Jonathan can see clearly through the crystal blue water as the sun shines right through the surface. The group begins to swim upwards. The goblins did not follow them into the water. Instead, they are firing arrows at them from land; however, their initial arrows all miss. The goblins mutter something to themselves, then take aim and fire again…

"Get down!" Dango yells.

They all dive under the water as the arrows hit the surface and sink harmlessly. Jonathan has to bite his tongue;

he wants to shout as the cold water is piercing the wound from the arrow. Again, the group emerges from the water and begins swimming in the opposite direction. Dango, who is continually looking back to check for the arrows, notices that one of the goblins is missing. Dango stops swimming as he tries to locate the missing goblin.

Dango thinks to himself that the goblin couldn't have gone into the water. Goblins don't swim, at least he doesn't think that they do. The group can see the land ahead of them as they get closer to the opposite side of the lake. Jonathan is wincing from pain as the cold water continues to hit the wound, hurting his injured leg. The goblin stranded behind them is still firing arrows at them, although the group is so far away now that none of the arrows even come close to hitting them.

As the group of rebels near the land, they speed up at the sight of dirt. Jonathan, especially, rushes as the injuries are really starting to bother him now. From behind a tree, the second goblin appears and begins firing at them, successfully flanking them. The group stops swimming and dives underwater. As the goblin reloads the bow, they rise back up for air.

"What do we do, Skrinner?" Dango asks.

"Skrinner!" Nox yells, diverting the attention of the group.

Three werewolves join the goblin that flanked them. The pasty goblin lets out a small smirk as the werewolves are almost drooling.

"Swim back to the other side; it's our best hope," Skrinner says as they turn to swim back. Jonathan is still wincing from the pain; the arrow in his right thigh is now loosely hanging from the mouth of the wound. The isolated goblin is sneering at them as he fires an arrow, which lands a couple of feet ahead of Skrinner, who is leading the group.

"He's toying with us; they know they have us surrounded," Nox reveals.

"I know. Avoid the noise. Keep swimming," Skrinner says as he continues trudging through the water.

They are now within easy striking distance for either goblin. The goblin takes aim directly at Skrinner. Skrinner is waiting for the arrow to be fired. As soon as the arrow flies from the bow, Skrinner ducks underwater.

"Jonathan, duck!" Nox yells.

Jonathan instantly pulls himself underwater. An arrow follows him shortly, and it digs into his right shoulder. The impact of the water lessens the blow; however, it still connects cleanly with flesh. Jonathan again bites his tongue to avoid yelling out in pain. While focusing on not shouting in pain, Jonathan is now slowly sinking underneath the pressure of the water and the pain from his injuries. Skrinner dives in and pulls Jonathan up to the surface.

"Is he ok?" Nox says.

"No, he's been hit again. We need to get out of here," Skrinner says as he struggles to hold Jonathan above water. Jonathan feels blistering pain coming from the two wounds caused by the arrows and his injured arm. Despite the pain, he can feel Mara's charm slowly vibrating and radiating a warm energy. The charm is seemingly reacting to his pain and is trying to help by providing heat, although it does not offer much in the freezing water. One of the goblins sets its eyes on Skrinner, who is now an easier target. The goblin licks its lips in delight as it readies another arrow. Just as the goblin is about to fire the arrow, an opposing arrow comes flying in from the left and rips cleanly through the neck of the goblin. Almost as if time stands still, the goblin reaches for the hole in its neck and then falls to the floor. From behind a set of trees, two women appear. One is holding a bow that is coated in a shimmering silver. The woman who shot the arrow is tall with a medium build; she has long blonde hair that is braided. Her blue shirt matches her piercing blue eyes, and her shirt is covered by a plate of armor. The majority of her legs are covered in armor, and she has a single black band tied around each of her arms. She wears a black archer glove on her left hand and carries a small sword next to her quiver of arrows.

Behind her is a younger girl who has short brown hair with jagged ends. Jonathan cannot see much of her from the lake, but her green eyes stand out for miles. She wears a blood-red hooded robe with her legs covered by shinguards, and she has a medium-sized scabbard hanging from her waist. She has two rings on each of her hands. She has a soft face with some light freckles. The younger woman has a belt with various pockets.

Jonathan is surprised by a buzz from Mara's charm, which he had forgotten was in his pocket. The buzz of the charm made him momentarily forget about the pain from the arrow. When Jonathan first got sight of the younger girl, the charm started to emit an energy. He cannot describe it, but the charm is radiating the same energy it did when he first met Skrinner.

"Enjoying your swim?" The blonde archer directs the question at Skrinner.

"Always a sweetheart, aren't you, Sera?"

"Always." The woman lets out a smile.

Sera nears the edge of the lake and extends her hand.

The woman behind her does the same. The group swims to them and gets pulled up to the sanctuary of dry land.

"What happened to the other goblin?" Dango asks.

"Flora took care of it."

Dango turns to the younger girl, who is named Flora.

"It is good to see you both again," Skrinner says.

The three men greet the pair of women with hugs and exchange some words. Flora introduces herself to Jonathan with a smile and handshake. She looked older from a distance, but now that he is up close, he realizes that she is about the same age as him. Or appears to be the same age; he cannot tell if the time difference between realms also affects aging.

Sera had not paid much attention to Jonathan; she eyed him over a couple of times. Finally, Skrinner calls Jonathan over and introduces the pair. Sera just nods in response, but she doesn't shake his hand or greet him in any formal way. After that, Dango, Nox, Skrinner, and Sera continue talking. Flora turns to Jonathan, who is a bit appalled by Sera's cold approach.

"Don't take it personally. She's like that with everyone when she first meets them."

"I thought I did something to upset her."

"She doesn't like most people. With Sera, you just have to earn her respect, which could take a while."

Jonathan just stares at her, a bit astonished.

"Took me a couple of years," Flora says with a laugh. Jonathan lets out a small laugh but winces as the reality of his injuries kicks back in.

"Are you able to continue?"

"I think so," Jonathan replies unconvincingly.

"I may have something to help." Flora opens one of

the many pockets from her belt and pulls out a small blue flower. She then holds it in her open hand.

"What is it?"

"It's a Nelle plant. It will help numb the pain for a bit. I have to admit it tastes absolutely awful, but it gets the job done."

Jonathan grabs the blue flower and puts it in his mouth. The plant immediately tastes stale and sour. It has a dry texture and is extremely hard to swallow, but Jonathan does it. Jonathan must have made a face of pure disgust because Flora started laughing.

"Like I said, it tastes absolutely terrible. But it gets the job done."

"Let's get going. All this action has made me hungry," Skrinner says as he pats his belly.

"Where are we going?" Jonathan questions.

"One of the rebel camps. I've been away for too long. Plus, you need medical attention." Skrinner gestures to Jonathan's several wounds which he seemingly forgot about while talking with Flora.

Chapter Six

After hours of marching, or what felt like hours, the group finally reaches the outskirts of what looks to be a makeshift village. The camp is surrounded by a tall wooden fence. From the hill that the group is on, they can see over the wall into the camp. At the very center of the camp, there is a big fire burning, and around it, a variety of tents. There is the sound of talking and laughing coming from the camp. Although they are still some distance away, the smell of burning wood fills the air. The Nelle plant had started working almost instantly, and the pain was subdued enough that Jonathan could walk this entire way without any real help.

"Is something burning?" Jonathan asks.

"No; well, yes. That is the smell of Ravibb cooking," Nox responds.

"What is that?"

"Well, food, of course! You'll love it."

The group continues marching forward towards the camp. The idea of relaxation settles in as they now see their eventual destination.

As they approach level ground, the fence now appears

much larger. As the group nears the camp, Dango, Sera, and Skrinner make their way to the front of the group. They stop a couple of feet away from the entrance to the camp. The entrance is a big gate, and above the gate stand two guards who eye them suspiciously. After some small chatter, the two guards move to the side, and the big gate swings open. The gate swings inward and reveals two guards who step forward, each of them with a spear and a holstered sword. The two guards above the gate draw their bows and aim them at the group. The guards who opened the gate eye the group and then eventually give a passing nod.

Skrinner takes the lead as the group steps into the camp, and the smell of burning wood takes over them even more. As the group enters the camp, the gate shuts behind them. Jonathan takes in the size of the camp as his eyes marvel around the complex. There are tons of tents, but there are even more people. There are warriors and what look like civilians; not only people, but Jonathan also notices some creatures and what look like elves, or maybe they're just people with big ears. There are children running and playing with each other. He spots a group of younger women and men, feeding some goats and other farm-looking animals nearby. The animals are mainly goats. There are about twelve or more goats in a huge pen. The goats look exactly like the ones from his world. That reminds him, how long has he been gone?

Jonathan's train of thought is broken by a golden fox that runs towards the group. Jonathan is spooked by it, although he does his best to not show it. The fox stops in front of them, and then, to Jonathan's surprise, the fox speaks.

"Flora, I am so happy that you have returned."

Jonathan nearly falls over in shock. Flora opens her arms, and the fox throws itself into Flora's arms. Flora then starts hugging the fox and talking to it as if it were a dog. Jonathan thinks about saying something about the absolute absurdity and just how calm everyone is about the talking fox.

"Yet," he thinks to himself, "it's been a long day, and a talking fox isn't the craziest thing I've seen today." The fox releases itself from Flora's arms and then gives a small nod to every person but freezes when it gets to Jonathan.

"Who is this?" the fox asks, perplexed. Jonathan does not initially respond. In fact, he is a bit frightened by the talking animal. The entire group waits for Jonathan to respond, and after some time, he steps forward.

"My name is Jonathan." The fox takes a couple of steps back and does not respond. Flora steps up to the fox.

"He's a friend; go ahead and introduce yourself."

The fox steps up hesitantly and prepares to speak, but then it stops itself. It then hides behind Flora's legs. Flora looks perplexed by this.

"I apologize for that; he is generally not that shy with newcomers. This is Sunflower." Flora gestures towards the fox named Sunflower. Sunflower does not speak to Jonathan; instead, it just stares at him silently from behind Flora's legs.

"Let us clean up a bit, then eat and get you some rest," Skrinner interjects, sensing the slight awkwardness of the moment.

Shortly after, the men of the group head to a nearby tent. The tent is basically empty, however, there are several buckets of water and rags all over. Skrinner motions to one of the buckets. Jonathan hovers above the bucket, which looks like a child's pail, given his height. Jonathan does not know what to do, but then he sees Skrinner take off his shirt and begin dabbing himself with one of the soaked rags. Jonathan has never done this before but decides to just follow suit.

Shortly after, they were provided with fresh clothes. Jonathan changed into a beige shirt and black pants. The clothing is really soft – softer than any material from Earth. While waiting for Skrinner to finish up, Jonathan takes a seat on a bench inside the tent. The tent is one of the bigger ones in the camp. Dango finishes washing up and walks towards Jonathan.

"Ever bathed like that before?" Dango asks as he attempts to dry out his hair.

"Never," Jonathan mentions.

"You get used to it."

The darkness of the tent is interrupted by two soldiers who walk in. They are wearing light armor and gray clothing. They step aside, and then a man walks into the tent, obviously searching for someone. Once the man enters, the two guards follow him as they walk towards Jonathan and Dango. The two guards have swords hanging from their waist, and the man between them is somewhat stubby. He is bald, and his dark skin contrasts with his light tan shirt, though not with his black pants and boots. The most notable feature about him is that he has a pair of axes, one each hanging from the left and right side of his waist. Each ax is engraved with gold and has chains dangling from them. The chains can be connected to the armor on his forearms, which would allow him to swing them and strike from a distance. No words need to be uttered; it is obvious that this is the man in charge.

"Karm. A pleasure to see you again." Dango extends his hand.

"Dango. I see you found some friends." Karm shakes his hand.

"It is a pleasure to see you all found each other again. And also, to meet the acclaimed Jonathan." Karm nods at Jonathan.

"How do you know me?"

"That is a long story. Which I will tell you, but first, I heard you are hungry and need some medical attention."

"Yes, we are all hungry, but Jonathan needs medical aid."

"How badly are you hurt?"

Jonathan raises his arm that was bitten by the werewolf. The wound is a bright pink color, and then he gestures towards the arrow wounds in his shoulder and right thigh.

"Wow, it looks like you had a rough first day. Flora told me she gave you a Nelle flower; that should numb the pain until tonight. Either way, once we finish eating, I can send you to the medical tent."

Soon, the group is reunited and sitting at some wooden tables that are near a huge fire pit. Now that he is closer, Jonathan notices that the fire is manmade and is there to provide warmth for the camp, but also to cook food. The fire is placed in the dead center of the camp in a clearing and, in a way, is the heart of the camp. A couple of yards away is a small wooden platform that almost looks like a stage. To the left of the stage are a multitude of wooden tables. Skrinner, Karm, Dango, and Sera are sitting at a table nearest the fire. They are eating and talking amongst each other; friends reunited once again.

Seated at a table further down are Jonathan, Flora, and Nox. They are served Ravibb in a small porcelain bowl that looks like it hasn't been washed in ages. Flora, however, assures Jonathan that it is clean; it's just the color of the bowl. Ravibb is a stew with chunks of meat thrown in. The meat seems to be goat meat, but Jonathan isn't sure. The stew is slightly marinated with some spices and generally tastes pretty good. Served along with the stew is a small bread roll that is a bit too hard for Jonathan's liking. Despite the unappealing look of it, Jonathan devours the food. The food is surprisingly really good, and Jonathan hadn't really noticed how hungry he was until the bowl of food was placed in front of him; so much so that Jonathan asks for another serving. The table has been awfully quiet until Flora breaks the silence.

"Why are you here?"

Jonathan looks up from his bowl. "I came to find my friend Stephen. But Skrinner told me he doesn't know where he's at. So, I think he is just going to take me back to my realm."

"When is he going to take you?" Nox butts in.

"Hopefully, soon. I don't know how long I've been gone, but I'm pretty sure my family is looking for me."

"Why don't you just go looking for him?" Flora asks.

"He's off with Rite training, remember?" Nox replies.

"Ah yes, I forgot about that. Maybe you should become a Myronid."

"I don't want to. I don't plan to be here for much longer," Jonathan says sharply, which effectively brings an end to the conversation.

After they finish eating, one of the servers brings a

round of ales to the group. Jonathan takes one look at the drink and immediately pushes it away.

"What's wrong?" Flora asks.

"I don't drink alcohol."

"What, why not?" Nox asks as he wipes away a drop of beer from his lips.

"I am not old enough."

"Old enough? How old are you?" Flora cocks her eyebrow.

"Wait, are you telling me you have an age limit in your realm?" Nox interjects.

"Yes."

"Wow, I did not know that."

"Yeah, so that is why I haven't tried it."

"Try it then," Flora says.

Jonathan grabs the cup of ale again. He stares down at the golden liquid and hesitates. Without wanting to look like a wimp in front of Flora, he chugs the drink in one gulp. As a small stream of ale drips down his lips, Jonathan slams down the cup and bows slightly to Flora. Both Flora and Nox applaud in return.

"How was it?"

"Not that bad, actually. It tastes like apples."

"I'm glad you didn't make the same face you did when you ate the Nelle plant, or else I would have spat out my drink," Flora jokes.

Skrinner walks up to the trio and sits down. He looks much younger now that he is washed up, clean from the usual layer of dirt and blood that seems to age him.

"Magiya would like to speak to you. He is attending to something at the moment, but he will call for you when he is ready. In the meantime, Flora can take you to the medical tent."

Flora nods in response. Once Skrinner walks away, Flora leads Jonathan to the medical tent.

Jonathan found out that there were multiple medical tents across the camp. However, Flora brought him to the one she usually works in. The walk to the tent wasn't that far, but it allowed him to learn a bit more about Flora. She is a nurse and healer, although she also occasionally goes out into the fields to help injured soldiers or spies. Once inside the tent, Jonathan sits down as Flora sprinkles some dust into his wounds and then tapes them up.

"What is this?"

"It is Crayian dust. It comes from a plant and naturally disinfects and heals open wounds. They will be sore over the next couple of days, but you should be okay." As Flora wraps bandages around Jonathan's arm, he begins to truly notice her. Flora has emerald-green eyes that are deep yet welcoming.

"How old are you?"

"What?" Flora asks, confused.

"Sorry, I just can't tell. I know time works differently here, but I am not sure how it works."

"Well, Jonathan, I don't think it is polite to ask a lady about her age."

"Oh, I am so sorry—I meant no offense."

"I am kidding, Jonathan, I do not mind. I am nineteen. I am not sure of the time difference either, so I don't know what that equates to in Yellow Realm years."

"Interesting."

"It surely is," Flora says as she stands up. She walks over to one of the other nurses and talks to them as Jonathan watches in silence. Flora returns and is washing her hands with a rag.

"You can spend the night here. There isn't a spot for you yet in any of the other tents, so you may rest here."

"I think I was supposed to meet with Magiya."

"Yes, he will send for you when he is ready for you. Feel free to spend the night here. Rest, Jonathan—you need it." Jonathan sits back in the cot and then lays down.

"If you need anything, feel free to ask any of the nurses here. There is always a nurse on duty. Until then, I shall see you soon."

With that being said, Flora heads out of the tent and leaves Jonathan alone.

* * *

Jonathan wakes up and jumps out of the cot. For a moment, he forgets where he is at. Once he looks around the tent, he is reminded of where he is. Jonathan does not remember falling asleep last night, nor does he remember dreaming. One of the nurses walks towards the startled Jonathan.

"Are you okay, sir?" the nurse asks him.

"Yes, I just forgot where I was for a moment. I do not remember falling asleep."

"The medicine you received is powerful and tends to drain your body's energy."

"Oh, that makes sense," Jonathan says as he looks down at his bandages.

"Mr. Skrinner came in here searching for you; he said he would wait for you at the camp mess."

"The what?"

"The mess, sir; the center of the camp, where the food is served."

"Thank you, nurse," Jonathan says with a nod as he walks out of the dimly lit medical tent into the bright sun outside. For a moment, he is nearly blinded by the sunlight. As Jonathan's eyes adjust to the sun, he begins to wonder if the sun that he is looking at is the same sun as his world. Before he can truly ponder that question, a wave of hunger hits him. Jonathan then regains focus and walks towards the camp mess.

After joining up with Dango and Nox, they eat together and talk. Dango takes another drink of his cof and then exclaims to Jonathan about his appearance.

"You look much better. And healed," Dango mentions.

"Thank you, I think Flora and the nurses did a good job helping me."

"That is good to hear. Would you like to train?"

"Train for what?"

"With your sword. Nox told me you weren't the best at wielding it."

"He shouldn't be out training. He has to meet with Magiya today and should be on standby," Nox interjects.

"That is true, but he could be waiting all day. A bit of training won't hurt."

Nox looks like he disagrees with the statement, but he does not respond. With that said, Dango stands up and motions for Jonathan to follow. As Jonathan leaves the table, he shoots Nox a sorry look. Now alone at the table, Nox looks at the pair leaving and then quickly jogs after them.

The trio are to the left of the camp on an elevated clearing that almost overlooks the entire camp. Nox is standing off to the side. Dango and Jonathan have their swords drawn.

Dango steps forward and stabs forward twice; Jonathan reacts quickly and blocks the attacks. Dango then takes a couple of steps back and lowers his sword.

"Now come at me, Jonathan."

Jonathan rushes forward and blindly swings his sword. Dango does not react fast but reacts smartly and blocks the hits while pushing Jonathan back. Their swords clash at the same time and nearly knock each other down. Dango is able to stay standing, but Jonathan falls back.

"You are naturally strong, Jonathan; that much is a given, mainly because of your size. However, your strength is uncoordinated. If you can control that, you will be a great fighter."

"Why are you teaching me all this?"

"We don't know how long you will be here, but there won't always be one of us to save you from enemies. You need to be able to fight off an attacker, enough to at least get you to safety."

"Do not train this boy to become one of those cult warriors." Nox steps forward.

"I am not training him for that, Nox. Why are you so cautious over this?"

Nox steps right in front of Dango and whispers something to him. The whole time, Dango is slowly shaking his head in disapproval.

"That was something I had no say in, Nox, you know that. Stop scaring the boy; I am simply teaching him how to protect himself."

"What did you mean by a cult warrior?"

"Nox fears that I am setting you up to become a Myronid."

"What is so bad about that?" Dango and Nox stare at Jonathan, astonished.

"You want to become a Myronid?" Nox says as he steps forward.

"No, I don't. I am just asking why it is so bad."

"It isn't – it is actually a great honor to train and become a Myronid," Dango mentions.

"They are rare for a reason; not just anyone can become one," Nox says. "They are powerful warriors aided by their crystals, and overall, are strong leaders."

"Then why doesn't the rebellion just get more Myronids to fight and end this war?" Jonathan asks.

"The Myronids were always few and far between, but especially so since the fall of the Republic. There simply aren't enough of them, no matter how powerful they are individually. At the height of the Republic, there were a good number of them, but now only one remains."

"What happened to them?"

"They were all killed. When the Republic was destroyed, the Anarchy of Powers made it a mission to hunt all Myronids. The Empire later wiped out most of their kind," Nox explains.

"Why were they hunted so much?" Jonathan says as he blocks a swing from Dango.

"When the Republic was starting to fall, the leader of the Myronids committed treason to the beliefs of the Myronids. Many of his members turned on him. This, combined with the fall of the Republic, led to a civil war among them. Many Myronids turned and aligned themselves with the Anarchy of Powers and helped create the powerful Mangalum."

"They turned on each other?"

"Yes, it was for many reasons that they turned on each other. But many believe that the Myronids planned the fall of the Republic so that they could take over."

"Oh, come on, Nox. Don't feed him those lies," Dango intervenes.

"It is the truth. The Myronids lost their way and became solely focused on control and power. Which is why I joined the Rebellion; to fight against tyranny and bring peace to the innocent."

"Wait, but if the Myronids wanted control, you're saying you turned against them?"

"In many ways, yes. I was one of the original senators who was against the idea of having the Myronids in the government. My allegiance has always been to a strong central government that provides peace, order, and justice to every citizen. The Republic, in a last-ditch dying effort to save itself, brought on the Myronids for security. The Myronids had always aided the Republic but never got involved in politics. Once they did, the flaws of the government were evident to everyone, and this led to the Anarchy of Powers. At the end of the day, they had as much blood on their swords as the Imperials."

"And the Myronids just wanted control? What if they wanted to help?"

"Once the Anarchy of Powers started infiltrating the Republic, many of the Myronids believed that the senators aligned themselves with the Anarchy and were trying to push them out. Some members of the Mangalum joined the Anarchy. Added to the controversy in the ranks of the Myronids, it all led to corruption and destruction. The Myronids took it as a betrayal. Once the Republic officially fell, a rebellion was formed. The rebellion that we are a part of now is trying to restore the Republic and give a voice back to the people. The Anarchy kept on and eventually formed the seeds of the Empire. The Myronids fought and, at one point, even tried to seize control of the realm themselves."

"Don't believe everything he says, Jonathan. He is just a bitter politician," Dango remarks.

"A bitter man who tells the truth. The Myronids are not to be trusted. I was one of the few who voted for the Republic to distance themselves from the Myronids. I was against the idea of bringing Rite into the Rebellion. I believe once he has built his forces up, he will turn on us and attempt to seize control just like before."

"But surely things have changed since then," Jonathan says.

"Maybe, maybe not. But the Myronids helped destroy everything I ever knew; therefore, I do not trust Rite or your friend, and if you would ever become one of them, I would not trust you."

"Stephen is not like that. I know that better than anyone."

"With the time difference, you may not have seen him in years. Surely, he could have changed."

"Nox, that is enough," Dango says, aggressively, as he walks over to the sullen Jonathan.

"Don't listen to him. Stephen is a good person."

"Thanks," Jonathan says quietly.

"No problem. You are unaware of this realm, and it would be wrong for someone like Nox to take advantage of your lack of knowledge and force his biased perspective on you."

"I am sorry, Jonathan. I do not mean to come off as imposing or hostile. I only intend to tell you the truth about this realm without the bias of being friends with the Myronids," Nox says, with a slight insult to Dango. Dango ignores him and does not respond. Instead, Dango swings his sword at Jonathan, hoping to catch him off guard. Jonathan unconsciously responds and brings his sword up to block the incoming attack.

"Good."

The conversation is interrupted by Skrinner calling Jonathan over. Skrinner is standing by the table as Jonathan arrives.

"Magiya is ready for you now," Skrinner says.

"Okay, I am a bit nervous, but I am ready," Jonathan says as he puts his sword away. As the two of them begin walking towards Magiya, Nox calls out to Jonathan.

"Jonathan!" Nox calls out again.

"Not now, Nox," Skrinner responds.

"It won't be long, Skrinner, I guarantee that," Nox says as he runs up behind the two.

"Make it quick," Skrinner says as he steps away.

Nox hunches over and grabs Jonathan by his broad shoulders.

With a hushed tone, Nox begins warning Jonathan. "Be careful with anything that Magiya tells you. He is a desirable ally to the Rebellion, but he also has a hidden agenda; he serves his own magic before the needs of the Rebellion. Do not let him test you."

"What do you mean?"

"He is a mage, so if he senses the magical potential within you, he will do everything in his power to keep you here."

"What magical potential? I don't have much. I didn't even know I had any till a couple of hours ago."

"Even if you don't, if they suspect you might be the Prophet, you will be kept here. If you are the Prophet that many believe you are, you are too important to the cause to be let go."

"Don't worry. No matter what he says, I won't stay here. Even if I am this Prophet."

With that, Jonathan returns to Skrinner. Skrinner waves off Nox, and they make their way through the camp. Through the maze of tents, they finally arrive at the only red tent in the camp. The tent is a blood-red color and is slightly moving in the wind. As soon as it came into sight, Jonathan could feel it. There is an energy radiating from the tent, just like the one from Mara's charm. Jonathan hasn't been able to place the energy, but he is sure he knows what it is.

Guarding the entrance to the tent are two armed guards. They do not move or react when Skrinner and Jonathan arrive. But it is evident that if anyone makes any type of threatening move, they will strike them down without a moment of hesitation. Their armor is straight black with a large red stripe painted down the middle of the helmet and chest plate. They have a large spear which they hold in their right hand with a medium-sized curved sword pinned to their waist, and on the opposite side, a small battle ax. Skrinner stops a couple of feet ahead of them and addresses them.

"We're here to see Magiya," Skrinner says with a slight bow.

The guards do not break their stance; instead, the one on the right simply nods. Skrinner responds with a nod of his own, and then they head inside. Jonathan isn't sure what to expect, but he can feel the energy get stronger as they enter the blood-red tent.

The inside of the tent is pretty empty. It is dimly lit with a couple of candles placed in each corner of the tent and the biggest candle at the center of the tent. Each candle is placed on the ground. There is only one small table inside. On the table there are a couple of open books, but behind the table stands an older man. He is wearing red robes that match the shade of the tent and the stripe on the armor of the guards outside.

"Jonathan, Skrinner… I've been expecting you," he says with a soft smile and nod of the head.

"Magiya, it is good to see you again," Skrinner responds.

"It is nice to meet you," Jonathan says as he bows. He isn't sure why, but he can tell that Magiya is not someone to disrespect. He cannot make out many details about Magiya's appearance. Magiya looks older and has a head full of thinning gray hair. He has a small face with a sharp nose and an almost sinister grin.

"Please sit." Magiya welcomes them with a show of his left hand. Then out of thin air, two wooden chairs appear in front of the table. Jonathan and Skrinner sit in the magical chairs. Jonathan wants to ask about the chairs, but he sits quietly without asking any questions. Magiya sits down across from them, and Jonathan notices the man's beady brown eyes.

"Ask me the question that is on your mind, son," Magiya says blankly.

"How did you do that?" Jonathan says, astonished.

"Well, Jonathan, I am a creature of many talents." As he says that, an apple materializes in his hand.

"Magic," Skrinner mentions.

"It's incredible. In my world we have magic, but it is all tricks. This looks real," Jonathan says, astonished.

"Oh, well, it is. See, I am a full-born mage. Many possess magical abilities like Mr. Skrinner here. However, every thousand years, a mage is born entirely out of magic," Magiya informs.

"You were born of a virgin birth?"

"Jonathan, that is not appropriate," Skrinner interjects.

"Nonsense. Let the boy speak." Magiya continues. "I had a mother, but when I was in the womb, for some reason unbeknownst to me, I was selected to be the Mage of this Millennium."

"That's incredible," Jonathan says.

"Now, it is no secret that destiny brought you to me for one reason, Jonathan. You came in search of your friend, Stephen."

"Yes, I did, but I already know that he can't be found and that he's off training somewhere to become a Myronid."

"Yes, that is true. But let me ask… if you did come in contact with him, what would you ask him?"

"I wouldn't ask him anything. I'd bring him home with me."

"And where exactly is your home?"

"Earth, the Yellow Realm," Jonathan says, although he knows that Magiya is aware of this.

"Did it ever occur to you that maybe Stephen does not want to go back? That he chose to come here, and that this is his new home?"

"Well, no, but that's impossible. He had a life back home."

"You are smart, Jonathan, but you lack vision outside

yourself. When Stephen came here, I sought him out because I sensed the magical power within him. I explained to him the importance of his potential, and he quickly agreed to stay; in fact, he did not even hesitate."

"You're saying he chose to stay?"

"Oh, why yes. We are not keeping him against his will. He chose to stay. He chose to train to become a Myronid. He wanted to leave the Yellow Realm behind."

"That can't be true; why would he want that?"

"Again, Jonathan, you look at his life from an outside perspective. To you, Stephen had a great life because you only see him as someone who impacts your whole. But you fail to see him as someone who is an individual. You may have had the perfect life, but he did not. He never felt at home; he always knew he belonged somewhere else. So, when he came here, he found his home. It's simple, Jonathan; he did not and does not want to go back."

Jonathan stares at the old man dumbfounded and speechless.

"That can't be right."

"Jonathan, I am a multitude of things, but I am not a liar."

"Then, I came here for no reason?"

Skrinner shifts in his chair uncomfortably.

"It seems so," Magiya responds.

"Why did you bring me here?" Jonathan questions Skrinner.

"You are important to our cause. You are the Prophet."

"No! I'm not. Can you just take me home? This is all a big misunderstanding, and I've been gone for too long."

"It was not a misunderstanding, Jonathan. I told Skrinner to bring you here. I could feel your magical potential from here," Magiya mentions.

"No, I am not any of that. I am just a boy. I did not think any of this was real… you can't keep me here." Jonathan stands up from the chair.

"No one is going to force you to stay here, Jonathan. But given your abilities, it is vital someone talks to you about what is going on."

"Jonathan, sit… please," Skrinner mentions, but Jonathan does not sit.

"No, I am not listening to this anymore. I am not your savior. I am not some magician or prophet; just let me go!" Jonathan says as he draws his sword. Skrinner stands up, shocked. Magiya does not stand up or even move from his spot. Instead, he flicks his hand, and Jonathan goes flying back to the edge of the tent. Jonathan freezes in midair, close to the edge of the tent, and his arm that drew the sword is pinned to his side. Jonathan is panting heavily as he tries to move or drop to the ground, but he has no control over his body. Magiya then stands up and walks towards the floating Jonathan. Skrinner stays in place and does not interfere.

"Listen to me, Jonathan. I do not wish to hurt you, nor does anyone from this camp. I have done vast searching, and I believe you to be the Mage of this current Millennium. I will not force you into this role. I seek only to warn you of what your life will consist of. You will be sought out by other seekers of magic. Many will try to use you, and some will try to kill you. You are generally safe in your realm, but if any capable being wishes to travel to your realm to hurt you, they can. You are a glowing light in the dark field of magic; many magic users can sense and find you without question. If you stay here, I will train you and prepare you to take my eventual place here amongst the rebellion. If you choose to leave, just understand you will never truly live a life of peace and that you and the people you love will always be in danger."

Although physically restricted, Jonathan is able to speak, but he does not. As much as he hates what Magiya is saying, he knows that he is speaking nothing but the truth.

"Nod if you understand me and tell me your choice."

"I want to go home," Jonathan exclaims.

"Very well," Magiya says and then releases Jonathan. Magiya walks back to his spot, and Jonathan drops to the ground. Skrinner rushes over to help Jonathan up, but Jonathan denies Skrinner's helping hand.

"I will send someone to fetch me an Orbitus plant; I have run out."

"A what?"

"The plant is what allows me to make an orb, as I'm sure you have seen. They allow passageways to open from one realm to another. But first, we have a visit from the local tradespeople. Let me attend to the tradespeople while one of my aides gets the plant. You both are welcome to join." With that said, Magiya ushers them out of the tent.

Now that they are alone, Skrinner turns to talk to Jonathan, but he just walks right out of the tent, wanting nothing to do with the man who brought him here.

Magiya makes his way to the center of the village where there is a crowd surrounding a group of people on a wagon. Skrinner and Jonathan follow along silently. Magiya's guards do not move and stay put, guarding the entrance to the tent.

The people on the wagon are dirty-looking, but that

is heavily due to their dark blue skin. Their clothes could barely pass as rags. One of the blue people is standing on top of the wagon and shouting what seems to be prices. The body of the wagon is littered with a multitude of clothing, plants, jewels, and even weapons.

"500 Cems for the tamwah hide!" the blue salesman yells.

A small group of members from the camp surround the wagon. The group instantly parts as Magiya arrives, leaving a clear path for him.

"Ah, Magiya. It is a pleasure to see you again, Sire." The salesman jumps from the wagon and lands a couple of feet in front of Magiya.

"Pleasure, Modrem," Magiya says as he bows his head.

"What can I help you with today?"

"Oh, I'm just looking, but I wouldn't mind an Orbitus plant if you have any."

Jonathan notices that one of the salesmen is constantly fidgeting. He has greasy black hair. This salesman has not looked up from the ground.

"Of course, I have a couple of Orbitus plants for my favorite customer." Modrem walks to the wagon and pulls out a brown satchel.

"Here are five of them, and for you, I'll sell them for the sale price of four." Modrem hands the satchel to Magiya. He produces four black coins seemingly out of thin air and hands them to the blue salesman. A rebel to the left of Magiya asks to get a closer look at the tamwah hides.

"Bring this fine fellow the hide!" Modrem snaps at his worker.

The greasy-haired salesman looks up in surprise and then rushes to get the animal hide. The hide is big and looks like it was taken off of a giant. The salesman, named Rodmer, brings it forward to the eager rebel. Jonathan can't shake the feeling that the salesman is watching him. As the rebel is examining the hide, the nervous salesman is slightly staring at Jonathan. The eager rebel is stroking the hide when he calls out.

"Tell me, Modrem. Do you heat your hides?"

"Heat my hides? Of course not! I am no conman."

"Well, this one seems to be heated," the rebel yells in response.

The salesman's face gets as red as possible.

"You must be mistaken. Let me take a look." Modrem walks towards the customer. Modrem feels the hide and then looks back at the rebel.

"The hide was in the sun, that is it." Modrem smacks the hide and then hands it back to the rebel, who begrudgingly hands over two bigger black coins. The salesman who is constantly fidgeting is now staring directly at Jonathan. Magiya steps up closer to the wagon to get a better look at the items for sale. Jonathan tries to shake off the uneasy feeling that he has about the staring man and steps forward with Magiya. Jonathan is looking closely at the items for sale; he notices similar animal hides, some minor steel weapons, dirty-looking clothes, and some minor jewels that radiate no magical energy. Jonathan quickly gets bored of the items for sale and turns to walk away from the wagon when he is tackled by the fidgeting salesman. They hit the ground hard, and the salesman pulls out a knife and tries to stab Jonathan. Before the salesman can even bring down the knife, the salesman is thrown a few meters away. Magiya stands above Jonathan, revealing himself to be his savior. The group of interested rebels all back away from the wagon leaving Magiya, Jonathan, Skrinner, and the tradespeople. Magiya then turns to Modrem angrily.

"What is going on Modrem?!" Magiya says angrily.

"We want the boy," Modrem says as he points at Jonathan.

"What business do you have with him?"

"The Empire put a bounty on his head so huge that it could feed my family for centuries."

"I urge you and your people to step back, apologize, and leave. I do not wish to engage in battle with any of you."

Modrem smiles and then reveals a red orb that is similar to the other orbs, but this orb is covered in fire. Magiya lifts his hand up to try to cast a defensive spell, but he is too late. The orb seems to explode, and a blinding red light takes over and knocks everyone back. Everyone in the immediate area is knocked off their feet, and those closest to the blast are covered in flames. Magiya was right near the blast but is mostly unharmed and is quickly getting back to his feet. Seemingly, the spell he cast must have shielded him from the explosions. Skrinner has some small flames on him but nothing major, and as he gets back up and draws his two curved daggers, he pats out the small flames. Jonathan is the furthest of the three from the blast and recovers fast, getting back on his feet. The entire camp is now on alert, and anyone who can fight is running towards the area of the explosion with their weapons drawn. The rest of the tradespeople have pulled out swords and are attacking some of the rebels. The tradesperson who attacked Jonathan earlier is now running towards him again. Jonathan sees his chance to escape and runs in the opposite direction. While running in the opposite direction, Jonathan passes by Sera, Flora, and Karm, all running towards the site of the explosion. Flora is the only one who notices Jonathan, but she does not stop.

Jonathan is running towards the entry gate. As Jonathan turns the corner, he notices that the gate is slightly ajar; the guards who normally guard it are facing in the direction of the explosion. Jonathan stops one step short of the exit and turns back to the site of the explosion. There are still some people recovering from the blast. Most of the rebels that Jonathan ran past are helping those who are injured, while the others are fighting off the tradespeople. Skrinner is locked in conversation with Karm, detailing what transpired. Magiya is just simply not there; at some point, he disappeared. Before Jonathan can think about his decision, he again notices that a crazed, blue-skinned tradesperson is following him still, except now another of the tradespeople has joined him. Jonathan turns and runs out the gate, not only to get away from his attacker but to somehow get back home.

Chapter Seven

Flora is the only person who saw Jonathan run the opposite way, and she eventually leaves Sera and Karm to follow Jonathan. Flora runs to the entry gate and notices that her companion is following quickly behind.

"Sunflower, why are you following me?"

"I cannot let you go alone, Flora."

"Stick close to me. I think Jonathan is in danger." The golden fox nods in response.

Flora turns to catch the attention of one of the guards.

"Guard, inform Skrinner, Sera, or Karm that Jonathan has left the camp and is being chased; also, that I am going after him to help."

"Certainly," the guard says, now noticing that the gate was not completely closed.

Once Flora and Sunflower exit the camp, the guard ensures that the gate closes completely this time.

Jonathan is running through the woods in the opposite direction to his arrival at the camp. He is unsure where he is going, but he knows that he doesn't want to be here anymore. As Jonathan is running, he can hear someone or something hot on his trail. With that feeling of being chased, he keeps running. As he is running, a number of emotions and thoughts come across his mind. Why did Skrinner lie to bring him here? Is he really part of this prophecy? Is he making a mistake by running away into a world that he doesn't truly know or fully understand? No, of course, he isn't. He doesn't belong here. He never did and never has. He has a home and a life back on Earth. The ground begins to get higher the deeper he runs into the woods, and he senses that he is coming to an elevation. As he is running uphill, Jonathan loses his step, trips over his own feet, and falls over. The force knocks him forward, and he rolls forward down the small slope. Jonathan rolls down slightly until he lands on level ground. He lays there and winces as he touches a couple of small cuts and bumps that the fall gave him. After some time recovering, he sits up and looks around the area. He couldn't have traveled far from the camp, but by the area, he can tell he isn't particularly close to it anymore. Jonathan stares at the sword that he was given, which is now a few feet away from him. A twig snaps to the left, and Jonathan rushes towards the sword.

Jonathan picks up the sword and stares at where the sound came from.

"There is no need for the sword. I mean no harm," a voice calls out from behind a tree.

"Who's there? Show yourself!" Jonathan yells, still gripping the sword.

A long-haired, blue-skinned man comes out from behind the tree. His black clothes are tattered in several places. His hands are raised above his head as he comes into view. His eyes are soft and also blue. Jonathan instantly recognizes this man from the camp—this is the one that tried to kill him. The moment the blue man steps into view, a small vibrating sensation fills Jonathan's head.

"What do you want? Why are you following me?"

"You sensed me? I must have been clumsy. Usually, I am unseen and unheard."

"You were trying to kill me."

"I was not, that was not me. I had no idea my colleague was planning an assassination."

Jonathan does not respond, but he can feel the magic trying to tell him something; he just keeps the sword pointed at the blue man. The blue man tries to take a step closer and steps on a twig that snaps. This causes Jonathan to flinch for a moment. In that brief moment of hesitation, the man rushes forward at Jonathan. The magic that was calling to Jonathan earlier now takes over him; Jonathan raises his arm forward, and through the tip of his fingers, he can feel an energy, almost electric, that sends the blue man flying backward into a tree. Jonathan looks down at his hands in disbelief; he has no idea how or why he did that. That light electric sensation he felt when he did that instantly leaves, and his mind is no longer plagued by that constant vibration. To his left comes the sound of several twigs snapping. Jonathan again raises his sword in a defensive stance.

"Show yourself!" Jonathan yells as he ponders why his magic did not warn him of this potential attacker.

From behind a tree, another one of the blue tradespeople steps out, both of his hands raised above his head.

"I am not here to hurt you, Jonathan."

"What do you want from me?"

"I came to help you."

"Help me?"

"I saw that he was after you, and I couldn't let him get to you, however, it seems you can defend yourself."

"Why should I trust you?"

"I could have snuck up on you while you were distracted or down, but I didn't."

"Why do you want to help me?"

"I have a son, and at one point he was lost. Some kind strangers eventually brought him back to me. I think it is amoral for my people to take a bounty for the Empire when we are supposed to be neutral in the conflict."

"How are you going to help me?"

"I am going to take you back home."

"You could take me back? Like right now?" Jonathan says as he drops his defensive stance and nears the stranger.

"Of course! I just need an Orbitus plant and some payment."

"I don't have any money! What is your name? I feel like I should know that at the minimum."

"The name is Chaviar. Anyway, how do you figure to pay for our little transaction here?" Chaviar is wearing a long black tattered coat, his clothes are all stained and torn, and he has dark blue skin that makes his yellow teeth stand out even more.

"Pay you? How? I don't have anything."

"I beg to differ." Chaviar smacks his lips and nods at the sword.

"You want this?" Jonathan places the sword in the scabbard.

"Sure. The metal it was forged from is of pretty good value, but I also want the charm."

"The charm? What do you mean?"

"Listen, kid, I am patient, but don't play me for a fool."

"Wait, how did you know about that?"

"Kid," Chaviar says and then solemnly points to the charm lying on the ground, covered in dirt.

"You can have them both. But you need to take me back as soon as possible, and no tricks."

"No tricks," Chaviar says as he lifts his hands up again.

Just above them on the ridge, Flora and Sunflower had just arrived and were hiding behind a bush. Sunflower is about to ask Flora a question, but sensing the question, Flora hushes him. They then focus their attention on Jonathan below.

"Why are you helping me?" Jonathan says, still suspicious.

"I am a gambler. I have no real ties; I help whoever can give me the best deal and outcome. Those buffoons that I worked with were idiots who shared the profits. I always did my own dealings on the side to get all of the profits for my family."

"You have a family?"

"Don't we all?"

Jonathan takes that into consideration and thinks about his aunt and uncle and just how worried they must be.

"If it's alright with you, I'd like to take you to the Orbitus plant now."

"Yes, sorry," Jonathan mentions as he snaps back into reality.

"Come on." Chaviar motions in his direction.

"Is it far?" Jonathan walks forward and picks up Mara's charm, cleans it a bit, then pockets it.

"From here? Not at all."

Jonathan takes out his sword, just in case. Although he

has a good feeling about the blue man, he still holds some suspicions about him and the entire situation. If it came to be a trick, Jonathan doesn't know if he could defeat the man. Yes, he is unarmed, but he may be stronger than he looks. But, in reality, Jonathan doesn't know if he could bring himself to kill a human. Yes, he killed the werewolf, but somehow, that feels like ages ago. Yet, this is different; this is a human. Well, a blue human, but a human, nonetheless.

Once the pair are a few feet ahead, Flora turns to Sunflower.

"Go back to the camp, tell Sera and Skrinner what just transpired."

"Yes. Yes, of course. But why do you need me to tell them?"

"I'm going after them." Hope shines in her green eyes.

"You cannot be serious," the fox says, sternly.

"But I am. I think Jonathan might be in danger; if I leave him unsupervised, that might be the end for him."

"You think Chaviar is setting up a trap to trick Jonathan?"

"Yes, he said it himself, he is in it for the best deal for himself. Turning in Jonathan to the Empire could lead to a huge reward for himself."

"But if it is a trap, what will Chaviar do when he sees you?"

"He won't see me. I will stay back and only interfere if the situation is dire. I will follow them; if Chaviar is true and leads Jonathan to the Yellow Realm, then I will return. But if it is indeed a trap, which I think it is, then I will strike when the trap is sprung and return with Jonathan."

"I do not like this, Flora."

"I know, but I need to do this."

"Why are you doing this? Just leave the boy; he doesn't want to be helped. Why risk yourself?"

"I am not entirely sure, but you always tell me to help those who can't help themselves."

"Don't use my lectures against me, Flora. If I knew you any better, I'd say that the boy has your eyes like the ocean has the moon."

"Hilarious, Sunflower—always the poet, aren't you? But go on, and in a hurry please."

With that said, Flora rubs the back of Sunflower's ear, and then he breaks away and is off. A fox with a message. Flora watches the fox trail off into the forest. Then she focuses her attention on the pair and follows them deeper into the woods that separate the rebel camp and Thead, the capital of the Red Realm Empire.

Chapter Eight

After a bit of walking through the vast trees, Chaviar and Jonathan arrive at a small clearing. The clearing is pretty empty besides a small cabin in the center that is flanked by a small garden. The duo walk to the side of the cabin and arrive at the fairly small garden. This garden only has one type of flower. The flower is notoriously known as the Orbitus plant. There are maybe hundreds of these plants, the source of the various orbs that are used for traveling amongst and between the realms. The flower is rather small; the gel-like sphere which is the orb hangs from the face of the plant. Jonathan can feel the energy—no, not energy but magic—which radiates from the plants. It isn't as strong as the magic that radiates from Magiya's tent or Mara's charm, but it's present and fulfilling. As Chaviar and Jonathan get to the edge of the garden, the orbs of the plants appear simple, almost beautiful. The orbs are clear and contain a clear liquid inside that rushes around the orb. The skin of the orb is soft to the touch and can be easily broken if squeezed too hard.

"Where are these plants from?" Jonathan says in amazement.

"No one really knows where they come from. Most of the time, beings of magic have them, but I am not sure where they get them from," Chaviar responds.

"How do they grow?"

"That I don't know as well; I assume from seeds like normal plants. But with magic, you never really know."

"Who owns the garden?"

"Technically, no one. At least, not anymore. The cabin and garden belonged to Heathon, the last official leader of the Myronids."

For an unknown reason, when the name Heathon was spoken, it sent a chill down Jonathan's spine. Not only that, but Jonathan felt the magic in the air stir up when the name was mentioned.

"The Myronids lived away from the Republic?"

"No. See, I don't know much about the Myronids or their history, but what I heard from others is that Heathon committed treason against the clan. Heathon was a great leader and Myronid, but rumor has it that he had a lover. He lived with her until he was hunted down and killed for breaking the sacred laws of the Myronids."

"The Myronids couldn't marry?"

"I believe they could, but not while serving, especially while being the leader of the clan. But that's enough of a history lesson. Get the orb," Chaviar commands.

"What do you mean?"

"Grab the orb."

"Why don't you? I don't really know how to."

"I cannot. The orbs, although they seem normal, are still creations of magic, and if a non-magical being touches it, it will burn my hand."

"What do I need to do?"

"I am not too sure. I think you just grab it. While you do that, I am going to use the latrine."

With that, Chaviar heads off into the cabin and leaves Jonathan alone with the Orbitus plants. Jonathan still isn't sure why the name Heathon stirred the magic around him. Was it the name or the cabin itself? Or was it the Orbitus plants? Could their magical energy be so powerful that it takes over the entire area?

Jonathan squats in front of one of the plants. The plant itself is a pale-yellow color. The orb must be heavier than the plant since the plant hangs forward due to the weight of the orb. The skin of the orb seems to have sprinkles of color in it, similar to the colors in the skin of a balloon. The magical energy radiates between the orb and Jonathan. He isn't sure how to tame the heat that protects the orb. Without much thought, Jonathan reaches out and grips the orb. He then tugs on it slightly, expecting some resistance, but the orb easily comes off from the body of the plant. The orb doesn't burn his hand, so either Chaviar was lying, or he is indeed a magical being. The sprinkles of color inside the orb seem to shimmer, each color getting its own second of fame.

Jonathan feels the connection; the magical energy that flows from him connects instantly to the globelike orb in his hand. A small spark lights between his hand and the orb. Jonathan is unaware of it, but he could easily use the orb to find his own way home. Jonathan stands up and looks towards the cabin waiting for Chaviar, but he doesn't see him; he must still be in the cabin. The sound of metal clanking together comes from behind the cabin. Jonathan turns around to uncover a group of about seven soldiers and creatures marching towards him. The group includes two goblins wearing light armor that is painted black, with bows like the ones that were chasing him earlier, a lycan that is standing on its hind legs, and a skinny wolf that looks like a mixture of a frail goblin and a woman. The creature has long thin black hair that is spread all across its unnatural head, and it has the face of a human but with a deformed nose and mouth. It is wearing a tattered white gown and has two small wings protruding from its back. The Red Realm Imperial Army is home to many hellish creatures and humans, but nothing could prepare Jonathan for the leader of this group.

There he stands, in all his psychotic might. Arma, a highly esteemed General of the Red Realm Empire. Arma is a freakishly tall, dirty blonde man. His blonde hair would shine in the light if it wasn't for all the stains of blood caked into it. His face is round, with piercing blue eyes and a number of scars decorating it. Arma has two large red lines painted over his face which part at the eyes. He wears a puffy blue robe that is tied at the waist by a brown rope, and brown boots dot his feet. Arma's blue eyes stare at Jonathan as he lets out a sinister smile.

Jonathan lightly touches the hilt of his sword.

"I wouldn't try that if I was you," Arma smiles. Hidden behind his smile is pure burning rage.

Jonathan's hand retreats.

"Good choice… we wouldn't want to get blood all over the beautiful flowers," Arma says as he playfully strokes the orb from one of the plants. Jonathan thinks about drawing his sword and attacking the unsuspecting man, but he has a feeling that the blonde man is leaving himself vulnerable on purpose as if inviting an attack. Jonathan notices that the other soldiers, who seem to take orders from the blonde man, are closely watching him.

The blonde man turns his attention back to Jonathan. He extends his right hand forward.

"Would you care to make this easier on my tired soldiers and turn your weapon over?"

Jonathan takes note that the man is missing two fingers on his right hand.

"Who are you?"

"The name is Arma."

"What do you want from me?"

"We want you."

"How did you find me?"

"You're not a hard person to find."

"Chaviar!" Jonathan screams, hoping his newfound ally can save him. But then all hope disappears as Chaviar appears from behind the cabin with his hands raised.

"I see you have met our paid associate."

"You work for them?" Jonathan asks Chaviar. Chaviar doesn't answer right away.

"Oh no, he sold you to us," Arma says as he pulls out a small knife from his blue robe and licks the blade manically.

"It's part of the deal, kid. Sorry," Chaviar says, somewhat ashamedly.

"Arrest our friend here," Arma says to his guards.

As the two armored soldiers step forward, Jonathan draws his sword and faces the group.

"Ha! Let us avoid any unnecessary fights now, boy," Arma says.

Jonathan shoots a glance at Chaviar.

"You said you wouldn't hurt him," Chaviar chimes in.

"We won't. But if he wants a fight, we will give him one."

"Put the sword away," Chaviar directs Jonathan.

Jonathan hesitates, gripping the sword tightly in his hand, eyeing his enemies.

"It is best if you want to live," Chaviar mentions.

Jonathan eyes the traitor and then the soldiers. He then slowly puts the sword away and offers his wrists to the soldier, who handcuffs them. The soldiers clamp some chains around Jonathan's wrists and then pull him forward. They begin walking forward with their newfound prisoner. As they pass by, Chaviar slightly hangs his head.

"Why did you do this?" Jonathan says as he begins to realize he was tricked once again.

"I told you. I am always in search of the best deal, no matter the cost. Sorry, kid," Chaviar says without making eye contact.

"I'll get you back for this."

"When will I receive my payment?" Chaviar asks, ignoring Jonathan's remark.

"I can give it to you once we get back to Thead. But you need to come with us," Arma mentions.

"As you wish."

"Good. Now, handcuff him!"

"What? Why?" Chaviar says, surprised.

Arma stands directly in front of Chaviar, and with a smile, he says, "Let's just say you aren't that trusted in the realm."

"I can't see why," Jonathan inserts.

"Ha!" Arma breaks into a hysterical laugh. "This one has some jokes."

"Very well," Chaviar says as he surrenders himself.

The group pushes the prisoners to the front and makes them lead the group. They then begin walking towards Thead, the capital of the Red Realm Empire. As the group gets clear of the cabin and enters back into the grip of the woods, Jonathan begins to fear that he has made a big mistake.

Flora, who was watching all of this transpire while hidden behind a large stone, begins to slightly panic. Her hand is tightly gripping her sword, and she watches on silently as the group moves further away. Without another thought, Flora draws her sword, exits from behind the stone, and gets ready to strike.

Chapter Nine

Flora rushes up quickly and cuts across the back of one of the goblins. The other goblin turns to retaliate but is cut down by Flora before it can respond. The skinny creature in the tattered white gown jumps forward and unleashes a hellish yet powerful screech that sends Flora on her back. Flora reacts quickly and throws her sword at the howling banshee. It stabs lightly into the skin of the banshee, so Flora runs forward and tackles the creature. She pulls out the sword and stabs it directly into the neck of the howling creature, the blade cutting the howling screech short. Flora retrieves her sword and stands back up to face the other assailants.

"Woah, woah, slow down, big girl," Arma says as he shows her his knife kissing the neck of Jonathan.

"Arma, it's been a while since I've seen your pretty face."

"Charming as usual. Tell the others to call off their attack, or the boy dies."

"I came alone. And I have no interest in the wellbeing of the boy."

"That is a lie. Why risk your life for him, then?"

"You are an enemy of the Rebellion. And I will always jump at the chance to take an enemy down, especially one as vile as you."

"As vile as me? Flattery will get you nowhere, Flora."

"You don't travel alone anymore ever since we last met."

"Silly girl. Drop the sword, and you both will live; you have my word."

"How can I trust your word?"

"Ha! You're right, you can't. But you have a better chance of trusting me than fighting me."

Flora eyes the enemies as if calculating her chances and then puts her sword away.

"Handcuff her!" Arma yells with a sly smile.

One of the human soldiers comes forward and places metal restraints around Flora's wrists.

"Why did you come for me?"

"I couldn't let you leave, Jonathan."

"You should've, because now we're both going to die."

"Oh no, you will die. The boy is a special request from our Empress," Arma butts in.

"The only one who is going to die is you, Arma."

"Feisty girl," Arma says with a laugh. "Keep an eye on her," Arma then tells the lycan, who positions itself behind her as they begin marching forward again.

After marching along for what seems to be hours, they stop and rest. Chaviar is leaning against a tree.

"Can't we use the orb to get there faster?"

"Smart idea, but I cannot use it," Arma responds.

"The boy can," Chaviar mentions.

"I don't know how."

"Yes, you do, and you're going to take us to Thead,"

Arma mentions as he gets closer to Jonathan.

"I don't even know what Thead is," Jonathan responds.

"You don't need to know. If you are as powerful as the Empress says you are, then all you need to do is think about it." Arma then proceeds to place the orb in Jonathan's hand.

"How can you trust him?" the one remaining human soldier asks.

"I trust the boy will not risk his life for any cheap trick. Is that right?"

"I have never done this before. If I mess up or take us to the wrong place, I may have just done it wrong."

"Any tricks and I will just hurt Flora, do you understand?"

"Yes, I do," Jonathan says, solemnly.

Jonathan can feel the connection form again between himself and the orb. He contemplates it as he juggles the orb in his hand. Thinking about his home, this could prove an easy escape for him. But Arma saw right through him, and Jonathan knew if he tried anything, it would only put people in danger. So, instead, Jonathan starts focusing on the name THEAD and constantly repeats it in his mind. While focusing on the name, he doesn't know how or why but he slowly squishes the orb until it bursts into his hands. Jonathan expects it to leave a wet residue, but the orb just disappears entirely. At first, nothing happens—no colored window to another place opens up. Jonathan is slightly relieved, glad to prove that he isn't that special after all. But then a red window opens up before them. The window is tall and wide enough for the entire group to fit through. Jonathan is distraught by this. He knows that opening that window means more than just a shortcut to Thead. By doing that, he cemented the theories about himself. A normal person shouldn't have been able to do that.

Arma motions to the lycan to step forward with Flora. As it does, the red portal slowly swallows the pair. Following them next is Chaviar, who goes in of his own free will. Then it is the human soldier who is almost cradling Jonathan. Lastly, Arma enters through the portal. A sea of pulsing red lights, the portal gives a warm feeling of air. Jonathan remembers this feeling in its entirety from when he first traveled to this realm with Skrinner, which now feels like ages ago. But this trip is much shorter, and in what feels like seconds, the group emerges out at the other end.

Jonathan is almost blinded by the low-hanging sun. After a moment, his eyes adjust to the dimly lit sunlight. The group is standing in dried brown-yellow grass. They are in a valley of dead grass and dirt. The valley is surrounded by hills on every side except towards the north. The north side is barricaded by a huge palace. To their left and in the center of the valley is a huge medieval-looking village with homes and people. A small amount of chatter can be heard from the village and a distinct smell fills the air. Although they are some distance from it, Jonathan can smell the firewood burning from the village. Jonathan can also hear the sound of children playing from the village.

"Who are those people?"

"They are the subjects of the Empire," Chaviar responds.

"Enough small talk. Blindfold them; they cannot see how to enter the palace," Arma commands.

Jonathan turns to the right to see the palace. At first glance, he thought it was a fortress, but it was not. The palace reminds Jonathan of the kind of castles he would see in fantasy movies. The palace is huge in scale, and the black stone that it is made from gives it the appearance of being made out of charcoal. Even a fool could recognize that this is the prestigious capital of the Red Realm Empire, the place known as Thead. The castle has very few windows and is built upward, but it also looks sturdy enough to handle any attacks. The darkness of the stones it is made from gives it the appearance of being fully black, but the closer you get, the more you realize the color is actually a dark gray. Jonathan didn't initially acknowledge it when they first arrived, but now he is starting to be aware of something. Jonathan can feel it – the energy and the magic radiating from the palace. It is like the magic that he felt from Mara's charm and the magic from the orb. But this magic feels different; it feels stronger and more possessive. There is an abundance of magic in the air, so much so that it is almost intoxicating. Jonathan has never felt magic like this before. His thoughts are cut short by a blindfold that gets put over his eyes, engulfing him in darkness.

* * *

Back at the rebel camp, the rebels are in a state of upheaval after the surprise attack from the tradespeople. Although it was a bit of a skirmish, the rebels eventually prevailed. Inside Magiya's tent stand the leaders of the rebellion: Skrinner, Karm, Sera, Magiya, and Dango.

"The clan of tradespeople claim to know nothing of the attack. They all say it was solely an act of an individual group," Karm mentions.

"Are we to believe them?" Skrinner asks no one in particular.

"Yes," Magiya responds. Skrinner is about to respond when Nox enters the tent.

"Sorry to interrupt, but I think you should all hear this."

"Go on, Nox," Magiya commands.

"The fox, Sunflower, came with an urgent message from Flora. He says Jonathan ran away during the commotion and was seen with Chaviar."

"Bring the fox in," Skrinner says with a hint of remorse.

Nox returns to the tent momentarily, followed closely by the golden fox.

"Is what Nox told us true?"

"Yes, all of it. Frankly, I don't understand Flora's sudden actions to help the boy, yet here I am, also helping the boy."

"Enough," Skrinner says to the fox. Sunflower puts his head down in shame.

"What do we do?" Dango asks.

"I believe Jonathan is in trouble. Chaviar should not be trusted."

"Excuse me, but did you forget my apprentice?" Sera says as she stands up, completely appalled by Skrinner's remarks.

"Yes, of course," Skrinner says, clapping his hands.

"I fear your judgment on this situation might be clouded," Sera remarks. Those in the tent are surprised that Sera so directly insulted Skrinner; all but Dango. Dango, who used to learn under Skrinner, knows that he can lack good judgment at times.

"What makes you say that?"

Sera doesn't respond but just stares directly at Skrinner.

"Tell me I am not the only one who sees it?"

"Sees what, exactly?" Karm asks.

"The boy. Jonathan… he's special. Magiya and I believe him to be the one who is set to restore the Republic."

The group all turn to the unusually silent Magiya, who just nods in response.

"You believe this boy is that special?" Karm asks Magiya.

"The boy is important indeed. Not just to the Republic, but also to the War of Magic."

"Is he the creation of magic?" Nox asks.

"That shouldn't matter. Please, Magiya, explain to my former master that this boy isn't worth the risk of what is to come," Dango beckons.

"We should send a couple of troops in search of them. I mean, they are both vital members of the Rebellion."

"He isn't part of the Rebellion. He himself made that very clear."

"You are correct, Dango."

"In fact, he seemed to want to leave."

"Ok, if we find them, I will take him back. We just need to find him and Flora," Skrinner mentions.

"I think that sounds fair. But only if their rescue does not require a war," Sera responds.

"Couldn't you search for them, Magiya?" Nox asks.

"I could. But if the boy has not used magic, I couldn't find him. Skrinner, do you know if he has?"

"To my knowledge, he hasn't. But if Chaviar took him to find an orb, I assume that he used Jonathan to retrieve the orb."

"You assume…" Dango continues.

"Yes, but that reminds me. Jonathan found a charm in an encounter with the People of Trent. You could track that; if he still has it, then it would lead us right to him."

"You're right. I will search for it. I need the tent cleared," Magiya commands. With that, everyone but Magiya exits the tent. Once clear, Magiya sits cross-legged on the floor and places his hands on his legs. He takes a deep breath and enters the mystical field of magic. At first, Magiya searches for the charm, but nothing initially appears. As he focuses more, a red spark lights up in the magical plain. The charm is in the Palace of Thead. Magiya can see it perfectly; it is situated on a table in an empty room. Interestingly, Jonathan is nowhere near it. He then focuses on Jonathan; instantly, his view of the plain is transformed into that of Jonathan in a dark room. He can feel Jonathan being tortured by a cyclops. While he is spying on Jonathan, he quickly peers into his mind, and everything that has transpired becomes known to him.

The cyclops brings the whip back and throws it forward as it slashes across the nude chest of Jonathan. He responds by yelling out in pain. The creature begins to charge up his swing again when he is interrupted by the armored guard at the door.

"The Empress has called for him." The words echoed through the loosely fitted helmet.

The cyclops stands Jonathan up and starts walking with him towards the Empress' throne room. Jonathan tries to take note of his surroundings just in case he escapes, but the beatings have taken a major toll on him and instead, he blacks out. The cyclops carries him the rest of the way.

Jonathan wakes up with a jolt. He is standing in a huge throne room. The ceiling and walls are incredibly tall and dark. A small number of flames light the darkened room. He can make out that he is in the middle. He checks behind him to find two doors just as high as the ceiling. Down the center of the room is a long blood-red carpet. The carpet stretches down the entire room and stops in the dead center where a huge throne stands. This throne seems to be made of the same black material as the palace itself. The throne is long and jagged, with the highest stone reaching about halfway to the ceiling. It is a huge throne, and any normal-sized human would look like a child in it. Jonathan is still a bit hazy, but the cyclops is walking him towards the throne. As they get closer, Jonathan notices two guards standing at the sides of the throne. They are wearing distinctly black armor with a large red stripe that is painted vertically across it. With those details, Jonathan knows that he has seen guards like these before, but his memory fails him. His train of thought is broken up by the creature sitting on the throne… no, not a creature, but a person sitting on the throne. The person is wearing a black robe that makes them look bulkier than they are. The robe has a hood, but they are not wearing it. The person's skin color is a mixture of dark green and light yellow. They have short dark green hair that falls lightly on their small head. The being has piercing blue eyes and lips darker than any shade of green. Their face is dotted with black dots that seem to form a pattern across their face. She isn't a big person but fills the frame of the throne perfectly. She is slouching on the throne but sits up when she sees Jonathan and the cyclops coming towards her. Now that Jonathan is a bit more conscious, he notices the magic in the room. This magic is similar to but different from that of the charm and orb. It is the same feeling that he got when they first arrived at the palace. The magic here feels even more possessive and seductive than it did outside. The woman in the chair stands up and claps her hands together. The cyclops stops Jonathan a couple of feet away from the bottom of the throne.

"Ah, it is about time I come face to face with the boy."

The woman takes the three steps down from the throne and is now at the same level as Jonathan. She did not seem that big from a distance, but now Jonathan notices that she is taller than him.

"I have heard much about you. Your presence has stirred me since you first arrived, Jonathan."

"How do you know my name?" Jonathan says as fear begins to settle in.

"I know everything and anything that I wish to know." With that, she takes a few steps forward.

"Your wish to return back to the Yellow Realm is misguided. You belong here. Your place in the story is here."

"I don't know who you are or who you think I am, but you're wrong."

"You are more important than you ever thought," the woman says. She is now only at arm's length from Jonathan.

"Let me go. I'm not part of the Rebellion."

"You don't know your importance, do you?"

"I don't care what you say. I don't belong here. I don't care about the Rebellion or any of this war. I can tell you anything you want to know about them, but you have to let me go."

"You rabid cur, you would stoop so low? Ha! You don't realize that we are completely aware of the Rebellion and all of its secrets. We know the location of their every camp. But we have not yet crushed them yet, because we do not fear them. Your minute knowledge of the Rebellion means nothing to us."

"Then what do you want me for? Why did you bring me here?"

"Your potential. I have felt it since you first stepped foot in the realm. Your magical presence disturbed me. No single person should cause such a disturbance. But you did; not because of what you are, but because of what you will become." Jonathan does not say anything in response.

"The last time a disturbance this great was caused was when Magiya was born. You are special," she says with a grin, her eyes admiring Jonathan as if admiring a beautiful flower.

"You're saying I'm the Mage of this Millennium?"

"Oh, yes. You are." Her evergreen lips stretch across her face with a sinister taste.

Instantly, it all makes sense to Jonathan. The whole reason he was brought here by Skrinner was because of his magical potential. That is why Magiya was so invested in him, and that is why the Empire is interested in him. This is why so much of this world has felt natural to him… because in a sense, this is where he is from.

"You must join me. Join us."

"No. I don't want to. I don't want this. I don't want any of this. I just want to go home."

"Join us. Forget your previous life. I can show you how to use your power and control it. We can become the most powerful mages in all of history. You and I, together."

"You're a mage too?" Jonathan asks, surprised.

"Yes. Two are born every millennium. One for either side."

"Either side? Magiya told me there was only one."

"There are many things Magiya says that aren't true. The Gorge creates two mages every thousand years to keep the ongoing balance or fight if you will."

"What is the Gorge?"

"The All-Being. Join me, Jonathan. Fulfill your destiny."

The woman reaches forward, and Jonathan comes gliding forward through the air. Jonathan is now directly in front of her, his face in her hand. Up close, Jonathan can see the black dots on her green skin are dotted in some sort of pattern.

"Let me go," Jonathan commands.

"Join me, Jonathan. Fulfill the destiny that was bestowed upon you." Jonathan can feel her rough nails slightly digging into his skin.

"Let me go!" Jonathan yells, and without much thought, he sends a bolt of electricity to her hand. She leaps back with a jolt and screams. After recovering, she looks at her hand and smiles.

"Cunning. If you will not join us, then you will die. Take him away!" she yells and makes her way back to her obsidian throne.

"Yes, Empress," the cyclops says and takes Jonathan again.

* * *

Back in the center of the rebel camp, Skrinner is rallying members of the camp. Magiya is standing with Skrinner on a stage in the center of the camp. Magiya had filled in the leaders of the rebels about Jonathan and Flora and their whereabouts. Dango makes his way through the large crowd awaiting Magiya's speech.

"Master, may we talk?" he says to Skrinner.

"Yes, but it must be quick," Skrinner says as he steps down from the small stage. Skrinner is now at eye level with Dango, the man who he trained and practically raised.

"Master, what are you possibly going to say to rally the camp to send an attack party to Thead?"

"Anything that has to be said, Dango. This boy is special, and he cannot be abandoned or, even worse, he cannot join the Empire."

"Master, who is he? Why are you acting so strange about all of this?"

"I will explain everything in time, but not now." Skrinner returns to the stage. Dango stands there, still confused about this entire situation.

The entire rebel camp is surrounding the small stage in the center of the camp. The crowd is unusually silent; they hardly call for meetings like these unless the situation is dire, and it must be especially so since Magiya is on the stage—he only appears there when something significant is transpiring. The camp sees Magiya quite frequently, but he usually sticks to himself; he hardly participates in the day-to-day affairs of the Rebellion. Although Magiya could be a useful weapon for the Rebellion, he knows his active involvement will create more havoc. If Magiya was to actively fight in the war then his opposite in the Mangalum, who happens to be the Empress, would fight back, and that could lead to a battle that could destroy all life in this realm.

Skrinner turns to Magiya, who then silently nods in response. Skrinner clears his throat and then begins:

"The leaders of the camp, including Magiya, have called you all here for a dire situation that could lead to the destruction of everything that we have fought for. Two of our own have been taken by the Empire. I know many of our own get captured every day and they are just as important, but this situation is different. One of those captured is Flora, an esteemed nurse and warrior amongst our ranks. The other captive is my new apprentice, Jonathan. Jonathan is our main concern at this point. I fetched him from the Yellow Realm after Magiya felt his magical presence. I brought him here, and after being tested by Magiya, it has become quite apparent that Jonathan is our next Mage of the Millennium. Jonathan is our Prophet who was foretold in the prophecies from long ago. He is meant to lead us to victory over the Mangalum and Empire, but most importantly, he is to lead us to restore the Republic."

The crowd was already quiet, but after hearing this earth-shattering news, they became silent.

Chapter Ten

Dango is just as astonished as everyone else in the crowd. Skrinner waits for the message to settle in amongst the crowd and then begins to speak again.

"We must deploy all of our forces to Thead in an attempt to rescue Jonathan and Flora. Jonathan is our greatest hope of destroying the Empire. We cannot do it without him."

Magiya steps forward to speak.

"I usually do not meddle in the affairs between you and the Empire, but this time I do recommend that you try everything to save them. There will come a time when I pass, and if you do not have a trained mage on your side, then you will surely perish. It is vital for the survival of the Rebellion that you save this boy."

"Saving this boy will win us the war?" a man in the crowd yells.

"Nothing is guaranteed, but it will improve your chances. You do not have to fight if you do not wish. It will be a bloody battle, as we are taking the fight straight to the heart of the enemy. Many lives will be lost, but I believe it will be worth it in the end. If you wish to fight, we will depart in about an hour. We hope to arrive just before sunrise for our attack," Magiya says.

"I will lead a convoy of my own, and so will Sera and Karm," Skrinner mentions.

"That will be all; you may all leave. The decision is yours to make. No less will be thought of you if you do not wish to join," Magiya says as the crowd disperses. The crowd is silent, each person contemplating the decision.

Dango rushes to Skrinner, who is already headed to his tent.

"Skrinner!" Dango yells.

Skrinner reluctantly turns to face Dango.

"Why would you do that?"

"I did nothing wrong, Dango."

"You lied to everyone. You made them think they are fighting to save the Prophet."

"How do you know he isn't?"

"Is he?"

"I don't know."

"Skrinner! You have risked the lives of nearly half of the Rebellion, all on a chance?"

"You don't understand." Skrinner turns away to leave.

"Then tell me, Master. I have known you for years, and never have I seen you act so irrational and impulsive."

"I do not wish to speak about this any longer."

Dango falls silent.

"We could use you for the attack. You could even lead your own convoy of troops."

"No. I will not participate in this. I will not lead our people into death on the potential of a lie."

"Dango…"

"Don't. I will leave to visit my parents at Riveren. I do

not wish to see the immediate impact of your actions on this camp." Dango walks away.

Skrinner is now left alone with his thoughts. It is a hard call, but it is one that cannot be passed up. The very fate of the Rebellion may lie with Jonathan, and to Skrinner, that is worth the risk.

* * *

Jonathan wakes up to find himself chained to a wall. The chains that bound his arms are submerged into the stone wall. He tugs on the chain lightly, but it doesn't budge much. Jonathan is trapped in a small circular room; it must be inside one of the palace's many towers. Flora and Chaviar are also chained up in the room, although they both look badly beaten and bruised.

"Flora," Jonathan calls out.

Flora stirs but does not look up. Jonathan continues to call her name, and she eventually looks up at him.

"Jonathan, you're back!" Flora says with some relief. "I thought they were going to kill you," she says as if each word inflicts pain.

"I thought so too, but I spoke with the Empress. Somehow, I then came up here. Are you okay?"

"You met the Empress?" Flora says, shocked.

"Yes, not by choice, but she wanted me."

"What did you tell her?"

"Nothing. She wanted me and my power... offered me a spot within the Empire, but I said no. Which is why I think I am back here."

"Did she torture you?"

"No. How badly did they hurt you?"

"Well, everything hurts, but I am still alive, so that

counts."

"Don't worry. I am going to get us out of here."

"How? Even if we escape, we won't get very far."

"I am not dying here, Flora. I need to get back home."

"You're right. I would rather die out there fighting for our freedom than rot in this cell."

"I got us in here, I can probably get us out of here."

"You're right, but how are we going to get out of these?" Flora raises the chains from the wall.

"Hold the chains out in front of you. I don't know if this will work… it may even hurt you, but it will be worth the shot."

"Wait, what are you going to do?"

"I am going to get you out of those chains using magic."

"Jonathan, I am not sure about this…"

"I think I can do it. I have been doing things that I have never done before. I should be able to do something this simple."

"All right, I trust you. But if I lose a hand, I'm taking yours as a replacement."

A fearful look overtakes Flora's soft face as she holds her arms forward, lifting up the chains. Jonathan focuses on the metal that binds Flora's hands to the wall. He takes a deep breath as he tries to tap into the magical energy that the palace is submerged in. Jonathan attempts to split the chains in half with magic, but it doesn't work immediately. Jonathan focuses on the chains again and mentally rips them apart, but again, that does not work. He lets out a sigh of frustration. If he is in fact the next mage, like the Empress said, then why can't he do this simple act? Frustrated with himself, Jonathan attempts it again. Nothing. Again, he tries, this time with a bit more anger and frustration, and the chains come flying off Flora's wrists. Jonathan lets out a small chuckle of relief as the chains smash into the floor.

"Jonathan, how did you do that?" Flora says with amazement, but her emotions are cut short when she sees that Jonathan also freed Chaviar. Jonathan then proceeds to free himself as Flora approaches him.

"Jonathan, why did you free him?"

"He is a prisoner too."

"He is the reason we're here!"

"He had no choice."

"Jonathan, are you crazy? He betrayed you."

"He had to Flora. He is a good person, I know it."

"Everyone has a choice, and he made his… now tie him back up before he wakes."

Before Jonathan can respond, Chaviar does.

"She's right, Jonathan. Restrain and leave me here. I do not deserve freedom."

"No, I am not leaving you."

"I turned you in, Jonathan. I sold you off for money and protection."

"Protection?" Flora questions.

"My family lives in a village near Thead. The Empress knew I was with you. That freak Arma threatened to kill them if I didn't turn you in."

"You had a choice, and you chose to betray him," Flora says.

"Flora, I have a choice too. And I'm choosing to help him."

"Why? Are you mad?"

"He is my only way home. I need him."

"Fine." Flora turns to Chaviar. "If you make any

wrong move, I will not hesitate to kill you."

"You do not have to worry about me," Chaviar says as he gets up from the floor.

The trio gathers in the center of the cell. The only light in the room is coming from some small slits in the walls. The slits are big enough for one rat to fit through, but definitely not a human. There is one bigger window, but it is still small enough that only a child could truly fit through it.

"Now, how are we going to get out of here?"

"Our only way out is to work our way through the palace, but I don't know where we came from. This place is huge; I fear we may get lost," Flora explains.

"I can navigate us out of here once we are in the lower levels. I have done business here before," Chaviar mentions.

"Okay, but what is our best option right now?"

"I don't know where we are. When I came here, I was never let past the entry hall. But I assume we are in one of the main towers. Usually, the towers are at the corners of the palace."

Jonathan walks over to the small window that is in the room, just wide enough that a child could fit through it.

"The window is too small, but a couple of feet below there is a walkway that I think leads to the other tower."

"Is it a big fall?"

"Not really; if we land correctly, we should be fine."

"Then let's jump," Flora says.

"None of us fit… didn't you get that?" Chaviar responds.

"Watch your tone. I know we don't fit, but, Jonathan, can't you use magic and widen it or something?"

"I don't know… to be honest, I don't really know how to do anything with magic."

"Then how did you free us?"

"I'm not sure. I just did it. It was more like a feeling rather than an action. This place is covered in magic, and I just tapped into it and had it do what I wanted."

"Then do that again, but this time focus on the window."

"Could I really manipulate matter like that and widen it?"

"Magic can do many things," Flora remarks.

"I… I don't know, but I can try," Jonathan says as he extends his hand towards the window. He tries the same technique as when he unlocked the shackles. As soon as he taps into the mystical field of magic, he feels an instant connection. Without command, magical energy shoots from his hand to the window, and the bolt of energy blows through the wall, leaving a gaping hole. The hole is big enough that all three of them could walk through at the same time. Jonathan turns to Chaviar and Flora, who are both staring in disbelief.

"Did you mean to do that?" Chaviar asks.

"Umm… yeah," Jonathan responds.

"Enough of this, let's go," Flora says as she runs toward the overextended window.

* * *

The march along the hills seems to have stretched on for days. Skrinner can feel the desperation of his soldiers as they continue on. Most of the warriors from the camp have decided to join the rescue mission, but once everyone who agreed to fight gathered, Skrinner began to notice just how outnumbered they would be. They had assembled a company at most, split into three platoons. Skrinner, Karm, and Sera all command a platoon. Skrinner has the biggest one, with about 35 soldiers. Skrinner and his platoon are leading the convoy, followed by Karm and then Sera. The plan they have set out is to attack the palace head-on. The Empire will not be expecting it, and the Rebellion hopes to catch them off guard. They do not plan on trying to wipe out the Empire or its forces… they could not even if they wanted to. Their only hope is to create a big enough distraction so that Skrinner and Sera can go into the palace and save Jonathan and Flora. But there are so many problems that can potentially arise. The rebels don't know where the prisoners are kept, and they only have a short amount of time to locate them in the massive palace. They know their time is limited before the Empire can fully defend themselves from the ambush. Once the Empire fights off the surprise of the attack, the rebels will be completely outnumbered, and that just adds to the nerves that fill each soldier's stomach.

Skrinner calls for his platoon to halt as they reach the edge of the Hills of Hell. Thead is a valley that is surrounded by three huge ranges of hills. The hills are dry and dead, and so is the valley, which is why The Elders titled them the Hills of Hell. The Rebellion decide to go for a frontal attack from the hill range directly in front of the palace. They know that guards will spot them, but the rebels prefer that they get spotted instead of attacking from an angle where they would have a disadvantage. The valley stretches out for some meters before the first section of the village. The village is rundown and almost looks abandoned except for a thick cloud of smoke that airs from the chimney of the centermost home. The Red Realm Empire has vast resources but very little has been given to their direct subjects. Those who live in this village tend to be the families of the soldiers who reside in the palace.

Skrinner turns back to his platoon, and he can see the desperation in each one of their faces. The Rebellion had been fighting a losing war for years, yet they never felt they had a real chance to win. But now that has all changed with the hope of their Prophet. The Rebellion has the opportunity to change the tide of the war if they can save Jonathan. Their faces are aching with nerves and a twisted form of excitement. A nervous soldier standing at the end of his squad in the leftmost platoon speaks up to break the obvious tension in the air.

"Sir, what are we going to do?" His teeth almost chatter.

"That is why we came up this way," Karm says as he and Sera meet Skrinner. "We attack head on… they won't be expecting us. Especially not at this hour. We will have a short grace period before they can send reinforcements."

"But, sir, the villagers," the nervous recruit mentions.

"Ignore them; if they get in your way or try to stop you, kill them. Send a message. This is not only a rescue mission but a message being sent that we are no longer hiding from them," Karm commands.

"But, sir… they are civilians!" the soldier cries back.

"War has many casualties; we strike at their heart and distract them. We won't readily kill them… only if they get in our way. Now, no more questions!" After saying that, Karm turns to Sera and Skrinner, who give him a slight nod in agreement. Skrinner turns to the village of people, hesitation slightly grips his throat. With a deep breath,

Skrinner draws his two curved daggers and points them.

"Charge!" Skrinner yells as he runs forward, leading the stampede.

The platoon rises and runs down the slope as they draw their weapons. Normally, the Rebellion would stage a coordinated attack, with archers bringing up the rear and swordsmen leading the charge, but they don't have enough troops for an attack of that size. Sera and Karm are watching the first of the troops reach the village. The first soldier of every squad in the platoon is carrying a torch. The troops start howling their most vicious war cries, and the squad leaders begin to set ablaze anything that they come in contact with. The soldiers are burning everything that they can possibly burn. In this case, most of the village is flammable. They attack while most of the villagers are sleeping, so many of them are caught by surprise. The other two platoons watch as the carnage ensues; innocent villagers run out of their homes trying to defend them but are instantly slaughtered if they raise a sword against the attackers. Skrinner feels a lump in his throat as he witnesses a soldier stab a young man who came out of his home with a sword in his hands.

"Skrinner. Call off the attack, they've done enough."

"We need to get their attention," Skrinner replies.

"They have done that. Karm tell him!" Sera pleads. Skrinner turns to Karm, who responds with a slight nod.

"The villagers will flee to the palace for safety. Have our troops prepare for their initial attack. I will take my platoon down with Skrinner's. Sera, once the Empire sends their first wave of defense, then and only then, send us your platoon. Do you understand?" Karm says coldly.

"Yes, sir," Sera says, almost reluctantly.

* * *

Jonathan stops at the corner of a hallway and peeks out. He sees the backs of two guards running in the opposite direction. Their armor slams together as they run, creating a sound of metal smashing together. Once the pair disappear down the stairs of the tower, Jonathan walks forward into the hallway. He motions for Chaviar and Flora to follow. Just as Chaviar steps into the hallway, a door opens, and two guards run out. Jonathan throws himself at the wall as Chaviar retreats into the corner. The two guards rush towards the same staircase as the other guards. Once they disappear, Chaviar and Jonathan step back into the light.

"Where are they going? They should have noticed me."

"I'm not sure, but something is going on," Flora replies.

"That's all the better for us. Now, let's continue," Chaviar chimes in.

The trio advances deeper into the palace. Jonathan is leading the group but truly has no idea what part of the palace they are in. Chaviar is next, and although he has been inside the palace, he has never been on the higher floors of the palace. Lastly, Flora is bringing up the rear; she is watching for potential enemies but also watching Chaviar. If he makes any wrong move, she will attack. Jonathan can tell that they are far from the throne room, which he suspects is towards the center of the palace, simply because Jonathan can feel the magic from the throne room. In fact, as they are sneaking around the palace, Jonathan is recalling his encounter with the Empress. The magic coming from that room is unlike anything he has ever experienced. In the area of the palace that they are currently in, the magic doesn't feel that strong.

They reach the staircase that the guards earlier went down.

"Wait, if we go down there, we might run into the guards," Flora says.

"Who says they're still there?" Chaviar responds.

"Where else would they be?"

"The guards went out in their armor, and they had weapons… they were probably called for something."

"They're attacking the Rebellion?"

"I doubt it."

"Then what is it?"

"I don't know. Let us find out. Jonathan, lead the way."

Flora gives Jonathan a worried look. She is still not fully sold on Chaviar and fears that they are being walked into another trap. Jonathan gives Flora a reassuring nod, and then he heads down the slim staircase. The staircase is small and barely lit; they head down in single file and take each step with care. Jonathan is leading the file, and as he proceeds down the steps, he can hear chatter and the clatter of swords from the bottom of the staircase. They stop a couple of steps before the end of the staircase, which leads into a small cave. The chatter from the cave reveals that it is full of people. Jonathan moves forward and peeks into the cave. His eyes are in disbelief as he sees a cave full of people. No, not people, but soldiers.

There are various creatures and people in armor all squeezed into the tiny cave. Jonathan takes note of one specific creature. It is wearing a dirty white gown that is tattered in many places. It has long black hair and has skin whiter than snow. It looks like a mixture of a petite woman and a goblin. It looks like the same type of creature that was present when Chaviar betrayed him. There are several werewolves and lycans in the cave as well. Some of the lycans are standing on their four legs and are snarling at themselves.

On a small ledge overlooking the army of creatures stands three figures. A wolf stands on its hind legs and has a metal chest plate. The wolf has a scar over its left eye. This is the same lycan that was chasing Skrinner and Jonathan earlier in the woods. Next to the lycan is Arma, the crazed soldier from before. Arma isn't saying anything; he is just standing off to the side, almost twitching from what seems to be excitement. Behind them both stands a figure in a black robe. The person is noticeably a couple steps behind the pair and is standing still. The hood masks most of their face, except the chin. The werewolf leader yells something, and the army roars back at him. With weapons drawn and spirits high, the army charges out the back of the cave. Arma, the lycan commander, and the hooded figure wait in place as the army leaves the cave.

"General, what is the plan of attack?" the lycan barks.

"Attack them straight on. We have no idea why they are attacking us, but we will make them pay."

"Very well, General."

"Lykos, leave no survivors. The Empress wants to send a message, but I want them dead," Arma commands.

The lycan commander and Arma head off, running into battle. The hooded figure follows after them slowly. The figure never breaks their stance or removes their hood. They just calmly walk towards the battle, but they never run or speed up their pace. Once the figure leaves the cave, the trio of prisoners makes their way into the cave.

"They're preparing for a battle. Is the Rebellion attacking?" Chaviar asks.

"I know you don't think much of the Rebellion, but even then, they would not be so stupid to attack the Empire head-on," Flora mentions.

"Then, who else would be attacking? Did you see the size of the army?"

"Stop it. We need to find out what's going on and how to get out of here," Jonathan mediates.

"I say we follow them and risk our chances," Chaviar says.

"Oh, you would love that, wouldn't you?" Flora responds.

"What are our other options? Stay here and wait for them to come back. We are in the heart of the Empire… we must act swiftly, or we will be dead."

"I agree with him, we cannot wait for them to come back. We should take our chances by leaving the cave," Jonathan says.

"I think we're crazy for this, but I'm the odd one out. Lead the way, Your Highness," Flora motions at Jonathan.

Jonathan begins walking towards the mouth of the cave. As he nears the mouth, the sound of clashing swords fills the air, along with yells of pain and cries of death. The sunlight blocks their vision as they exit the cave; although their vision is skewed, they can hear the fighting very well. The trio are about to walk into a war. Part of Jonathan wants to run back and hide from the war outside. Not only is he running into a war, but he is running into the magical force that is calling him. He can't explain it but, somehow, he knows if he walks out of this cave, his life will never be the same. Destiny is calling his name, and the decision is his to walk with it or not. He steps out of the cave into the battle.

Chapter Eleven

The sword cuts through the two Imperial soldiers. The Rebellion fighter turns to see more Imperial soldiers running out of the bottom of the palace. The sight is one straight from hell; there are a few humans amongst the ranks of the Empire, but it is mostly creatures. Creatures like werewolves, banshees, goblins, orcs, and elves. But the worst of the Imperial creatures is not a monster but a man. His blonde hair is caked with blood, most of it older than the day. He relishes his curved dagger as he extracts it from the head of a fallen rebel. This is what he lives for – bloody war.

The forces of the Rebellion and Empire are clashing in the dry fields of Thead. At this moment, the Rebellion forces, led by Karm and Skrinner, are prevailing. Karm and Skrinner are veterans of war and are striking down Imperials with ease. They are mainly staying on the defensive, only attacking when a true opportunity presents itself. Karm is a nobleman and leader, but he is a brutal fighter when provoked. Skrinner watches as Karm digs one of the axes tied to his armor into the head of a screeching banshee. He takes out the ax and tosses it at the head of another hellish creature. The Rebellion has control of the battle, so much so that Skrinner is unbothered as he advances slowly to the palace. Karm runs up to Skrinner, a tad out of breath.

"This is too easy. I have a bad feeling about this," Karm mentions.

"I agree. We can rest now, but a second wave will be here shortly."

"I saw Nox's brother."

"I saw him too… the years haven't been kind to him."

"Frankly, I think he enjoys looking like that."

Before Karm can respond, a loud whistle is blown from one of the Hills of Hell. They both turn to see Sera motioning to the opposite sides of the valley. That's when the tide of the battle changes. Flanking the Rebellion forces come two brigades of Imperial forces, one from each side, each brigade numbering in the thousands. Karm whistles a signal back to Sera to have her bring her platoon.

"Till death?" Karm says to Skrinner.

"Till death, brother."

"And may we take that bastard Arma with us."

Arma runs up to a Rebellion soldier who is staring at the oncoming forces. Arma stabs the man with his curved dagger and brings him down to the ground. He takes out the knife, which had only lightly pierced the man's armor, and begins stabbing him repeatedly. Arma laughs as he continues in his horrific act. Once the soldier is dead, Arma licks the blood on the blade and charges into battle again with the Imperial Brigades that have just arrived. The Rebellion forces are now vastly outnumbered, but they continue fighting, although many are dying.

Jonathan is caught between two charging Imperial soldiers who pay no attention to him as they kill the rebel behind Jonathan. Flora rushes to the fallen rebel and takes his small sword from him.

"This is a massacre!" Jonathan screams as he picks up a mace from a fallen werewolf.

"The Rebellion was smarter, you said?" Chaviar remarks.

"Test me again and it'll be your throat, zed!" Flora says as she points her newfound sword at Chaviar.

"Can you guys not argue in the middle of a battlefield?"

"Have him prove his allegiance to the rebellion, even if it's just temporary, or else I'll kill him."

Chaviar reacts quickly and stabs an unsuspecting Imperial in the back.

"There, Your Majesty." He cleans the sword on the ground.

Two Imperial soldiers run towards the trio. Flora makes quick work of one of them, while Chaviar struggles a bit, but then eventually rids them of the other.

"The Rebellion; why are they here?" Chaviar asks.

"I don't know, but I think I see Karm; we should work our way to him. Follow me!" Flora runs off, jumps, and stabs her sword into the neck of a werewolf. Jonathan runs up behind Flora and uses his mace to strike the wolf's head. The werewolf falls to the ground, and Jonathan can feel it again. The magic that radiates from the dead body.

Sera's forces arrive to aid a deflated army. The Rebellion forces are being wiped out easily. Her platoon doesn't give them many more troops, but it allows some of the more tired troops to retreat slightly. Sera spots Flora from a distance and charges towards her, killing any enemies in her way. A sense of relief rushes over Flora as she reunites with her guardian.

"Flora!" Sera welcomes the trio but never breaks her defensive stance. Together, they charge towards Karm and Skrinner, who are making their way towards them. The two groups, along with various other Rebellion soldiers, meet halfway.

"Jonathan, I am so glad you're okay, and you too, Flora," Skrinner mentions.

"Thank you," Jonathan responds.

Skrinner eyes Chaviar, but Jonathan gives him a small nod to show his approval.

"Skrinner!" Karm yells.

The group turns to see three new brigades coming from each side of the valley. These troops look different; they are all archers and are smaller in number.

"What are they doing?"

"Hellfire," Karm replies.

"Everyone needs to huddle together now!" Skrinner begins moving his fingers around.

"What is going on?" Jonathan asks.

"Those archers are going to fire at this section of the battlefield, killing us and the rest of their troops. I am trying to make a barrier for us, but the magic here is distant," Skrinner responds while never breaking his concentration.

Meanwhile, the lines of archers stop and arm their bows. The Imperial soldiers on the battlefield with the rebels continue fighting despite their immediate death.

"SKRINNER!" Sera yells as the archers fire their arrows into the air. Jonathan stares at the hundreds of arrows that go soaring into the air. He quickly turns to Flora who shuts her eyes, and then to Skrinner who is still trying to conjure up some sort of a magical barrier. As the arrows begin to make their way down, Jonathan brings his arms up and calls upon the magic that has been crackling at his fingertips ever since he entered the battlefield. An invisible barrier forms around the remaining rebels and any arrow that strikes the barrier is immediately disintegrated. Most of the rebels must have their eyes closed as they don't react immediately to being saved. After slowly realizing they are not dead, they begin to peek and suddenly realize they were saved. Then, their eyes quickly turn to their savior.

"Jonathan! How did you do that?" Skrinner begins to say.

As the remaining Rebellion soldiers prepare to fight again, they turn to see that many of the arrows had instead killed some of the Imperial forces.

"We need to retreat now before they kill us all," Karm mentions.

The remaining Imperial soldiers who aren't dead pick themselves up and charge at the remaining rebel forces in the center of the field. The rebels raise their weapons and prepare to fight. Sera takes down several enemies from a distance with her bow and arrow, providing some extra seconds of freedom before the clans clash. Quickly, the rebel forces are surrounded once again.

"Karm, what do we do?!" Sera yells as she fires an arrow.

"Retreat, we got what we came for." Karm nods at Sera and then at Skrinner. Almost in unison, the three Generals blow their whistles to signal for retreat.

With that sound, the Rebellion forces begin to run back towards the Hills of Hell. Arma finishes off a rebel troop and stares in disbelief at the fleeing troops. He searches the battlefield with his eyes for Lykos, his lycan

Commander. Lykos is struggling to kill a Rebellion archer. The lycan picks up the frail woman and slams her to the ground, then picks up his small dagger and ends her life swiftly. Lykos looks up to see the rebels retreating, then looks at the archers creating a perimeter around the battlefield. Arma and Lykos call for the Imperial troops to chase after the fleeing rebels.

The rebel forces are stopped; as they try to retreat, the wall of archers comes forward and blocks their way. The rebels try to run back, but they are being flanked by the Imperial forces.

"We're stuck, what do we do?" Flora yells.

The wall of archers arm their bows and begin firing at the rebels. This time not into the air, but directly at their intended targets. Jonathan looks around frantically as he sees several rebels struck down. He can feel this static sensation at his fingertips, and without much thought, he raises his hands. The magic shoots out of him, and he creates another invisible barrier that disintegrates any arrow that comes their way.

"Great work, Jonathan!" Skrinner exclaims.

"How long can he hold that for?" Karm says as he cuts into a werewolf.

"I don't know, but I can try my best."

"Cover Jonathan, we need to take out as many of the oncoming forces as we can. Hold strong, soldiers!" Karm yells as he throws his ax at a banshee. The Imperial forces quickly close in, and again, the rebels are cornered. Jonathan is doing his best to hold up the shield, but he can feel his strength draining as arrows continue crashing into the barrier. The rebels are still fighting, but they are quickly dying off; they will not be able to hold up in this situation.

Jonathan can feel his barrier getting weaker as the magic is draining him. He won't be able to hold it up much longer. Before Jonathan can warn the rebels about his weakening shield, he falls down. The barrier falls with Jonathan, and the arrows come flying through, instantly picking off a couple more rebel soldiers.

"Karm!" Sera yells.

Karm turns to Sera, who is pointing towards the hill which they entered the valley from. The sound of horses running fills the air, along with the ever-so-subtle sound of armor clanking together. On top of the hill now sits a battalion of troops in blue armor and on white horses. Each soldier looks well-armored and equipped for battle alongside a powerful white horse. Leading the troops is a strong-looking horse bearing a man wearing a chest plate that has an "X" smeared on it with blood. He has a long sword holstered on his back, long black hair, and light brown skin caked in dirt. They can see his green eyes from a mile away… Dango.

"Charge!" Dango yells as he points his sword toward the Gothic palace and rides into the valley with his battalion of troops following him.

158

Chapter Twelve

Dango rides down and takes down two archers with his sword. His troops follow, and they take down the small wall of archers blocking the exit for the rebels.

"Fight!" Karm yells as he launches his ax at a goblin that was focused on the other soldiers. The rebels begin fighting again; Sera fires her arrows, and Flora swings the blade she found. Skrinner is fighting with his favorite curved daggers. Flora runs to help Jonathan, who is slowly recovering from the magic draining him.

Arma works his way toward Skrinner, who is finishing a yellow-skinned orc. He stops a few paces in front of him.

"Skrinner, it has been such a long time."

"Arma, I almost didn't recognize you with the face paint and bloodstains."

"Still as charming as ever," Arma says as he plays with the blade in his hand.

"Your brother doesn't know you're here, or else I'm sure he would have joined us to see to it that you don't escape again."

"Those are big words, Skrinner. Make sure you can handle the consequences of them." Arma launches the knife that he had in his hand at Skrinner. Skrinner reacts quickly and moves just enough, but the knife still catches him. The blade disappears into his shoulder as Skrinner yells out in pain.

"I've wanted to do this for a long time," Arma yells as he charges at Skrinner.

"Skrinner!" Karm yells as he runs in and tackles Arma to the ground.

Lykos sees his outnumbered ally and charges towards Karm. The wolf gets there quickly and tackles Skrinner. Skrinner stabs one of his daggers into the wolf's side. The wolf howls in Skrinner's face. Jonathan runs and kicks Lykos off Skrinner. Karm helps the wounded Skrinner up.

Arma is watching them recover as he cleans his hands on his blue robe and stands back up. He pulls out a sword from his robe, and Skrinner recognizes it instantly.

"I believe you have something that belongs to my apprentice," Skrinner remarks.

"Take it from me, Skrinner, or pry it from my dead hands."

"Jonathan," Karm calls out and then tosses Jonathan a small dagger.

Jonathan steps forward holding the dagger, and Skrinner stands up next to him.

"Pick your poison, boy. The wolf or the animal?" Skrinner asks Jonathan.

Jonathan takes no time to think and charges at Arma. Arma retreats a couple steps, then laughs as Jonathan charges at him. "I love the fiery spirit!" Arma yells as he blocks Jonathan's first strike. Their swords clank, and Arma pushes Jonathan back.

"That sword belongs to me," Jonathan says as he recovers from the blow.

"You can take it from my dead body, boy!" Arma yells as he fakes a stab and then slashes Jonathan cleanly across his chest. Jonathan yells as he staggers back. The cut wasn't deadly, but it cut cleanly through his skin, and he is slightly bleeding from it. Jonathan feels the magic tingling at his fingertips. He raises his arm up and pulls on the magic that is calling him. Arma sails through the air and drops a couple of meters in front of Jonathan. Jonathan didn't use enough magic to pull him completely, but he still pulled him forward; Arma is shocked by this. Jonathan seizes the moment and slashes his dagger forward. Arma tries to bring up his sword to deflect the blow, but he responds too late. Jonathan's dagger cuts clean through Arma's right hand. Arma lets out a shriek of pure pain and shock as he falls to his knees. Jonathan picks up his original sword and points it at Arma. Jonathan feels the magic radiating within him once again.

"Jonathan, let's go!" Skrinner stops by Jonathan's side. Jonathan turns and sees that the Imperial forces are fleeing back into the palace. A small purple portal opens in front of Jonathan, and out comes the hooded figure that he saw inside the cave. They swipe their hand forward, sending Jonathan and Skrinner across the ground. The hooded figure stands near the wounded Arma and Lykos, and with a clap of their hands, creates another purple portal. The hooded figure pulls both Arma and Lykos through the portal.

They turn to see the army that Dango brought, picking up the remaining rebel soldiers. One of the armored soldiers drops off a horse with Skrinner. Jonathan turns to the purple portal and feels the magic radiating off it.

Skrinner puts his two curved daggers away and mounts the horse. Jonathan can feel the energy from the portal calling to him, but he puts his sword away.

"Get on, kid," Skrinner says.

Jonathan climbs onto the horse and admires the dead valley as they ride out of the valley of death.

Chapter Thirteen

T he Battle of Underhill was a brutal one with many casualties, but the mission was a success! We must mourn our losses but also celebrate our victory!" Magiya yells at the rebel camp. The rebels cheer, and then they continue on with their celebration. The fire in the center of the camp is burning brightly with fresh wood as a feast is being prepared. The camp is lively with discussions about the battle. This was the first time in this long dreadful war that the Rebellion has had a significant victory over the Empire. Many of the Rebellion soldiers believe it is the start of a new era in the war. Jonathan is conversing with Flora, who is chugging down a drink while Sunflower sits on her lap.

"What's wrong?" Flora asks as she sets her ale down.

"I don't know why, but I'm going to miss it here."

"But it's what you wanted, isn't it? You said it best; you don't belong here."

"I know, but I feel somehow connected to this place. Plus, I made some pretty good friends here."

"You made friends?"

"I think so," Jonathan mentions.

"Friends is hardly what I would call it," Sunflower remarks.

"I have something I want to leave with you."

"What is it?"

Jonathan extends his hand and reveals a necklace that holds a gold charm with a big evergreen emerald in it.

"It's beautiful," Flora says as she touches the charm.

"I know," he says while looking at her.

"But why do you want me to have it? Where did you even get this?"

"I got it when I first got here. I don't have much use for it back home. I felt the magic of this charm when I first came here. I think it should stay here with you."

"I am not a big fan of green, but I will hold on to it for you," Flora says with a smile.

"Flora, I don't know if I will ever come back."

"Well, if you don't, I'll sell the charm for a new sword." With that said they both break out in laughter, while Sunflower just watches them quietly. Dango, Magiya, and Skrinner arrive at the table that they are at. Jonathan makes eye contact with Skrinner, who gives him a look that tells him it's time to go. Jonathan stands up from the table.

"Goodbye, Flora. Hopefully, we meet again," Jonathan says as he slightly hugs Flora who is now standing.

"Till we meet again," Flora says proudly. Jonathan then turns to the golden fox, Sunflower.

"Nice meeting you. I don't think I will ever forget you."

"Do not try to flatter me, boy," the fox says, sternly.

"I didn't mean it that way; you are the only talking animal I have ever met. So yes, I will never forget you."

"Goodbye, Jonathan," the fox says with a slight smirk.

"It was nice meeting you; till we meet again."

"Goodbye, Dango," Jonathan says as he extends his hand forward.

"Goodbye, Jonathan," Dango says as they shake hands.

Jonathan turns to Magiya who is still followed by his two guards.

"Jonathan, you are now open to the world of magic. You helped save the rebellion and have given us hope unlike ever before. Stay vigilant and remember; in the face of danger, although the magical energy in the Yellow Realm is almost extinct, it is still present, and you will always have it at your disposal. Stay safe, young one… you are always welcome back." Magiya passes a brown bag to Jonathan.

"What is this?" Jonathan says.

"It is a trio of orbs. If you ever need to come back, you have your way."

"Thank you, Magiya."

Magiya and Jonathan share a nod, and then Jonathan walks off with Skrinner. Dango is left standing with Magiya.

"Will the boy be safe?" Dango asks Magiya.

"No, he will never truly be safe. He opened himself up to the world of magic—any being with magical potential could feel him. But I believe the boy can handle himself."

Jonathan and Skrinner walk silently out of the camp and stop in the field outside.

"I apologize for bringing you here without giving you every detail, Jonathan. I manipulated you, and I was wrong… I am sorry."

"Thank you for saying that; I accept your apology. I'm sorry for running off."

"No need to apologize for that; I was a fool. Are you

ready to go?" Skrinner says.

"Is it hard?"

"What? Opening a portal? For me, yes, but apparently not for you," Skrinner says with a slight laugh.

"No, I mean leaving."

"Yes, but it gets easier the more you do it. Listen, Jonathan, if you ever want to come back, you are welcome to."

"Thanks, but I don't really know how to find you."

"Once you use the orbs, just use magic to find me or Magiya. We will always be here."

"Thank you. I know I wasn't the best traveling companion, but thank you for everything, Skrinner. You blew my mind and showed me everything that I have always wanted to see. I can't believe everything that I used to read about was all true. You took me on a trip of a lifetime, and I will always appreciate that." Jonathan smiles and shakes Skrinner's hand.

"You're welcome, Jonathan."

"I am ready to go home."

"Very well," Skrinner says as he pulls out an orb from his vest.

"Wait, how much time has passed since I left?"

"Um, maybe about a week. I can't be too sure."

"Right. Time goes slower."

Yes, I hope you won't get into too much trouble back home."

"Only one way to find out."

"Are you ready?" Jonathan nods in response. Skrinner tosses the orb, and a yellow window appears out of thin air. The yellow window is slightly pulsing as it is illuminating the dark field. Jonathan takes one last look at the smoke coming from the rebel camp. He can hear the various conversations and celebrations. The opportunity for him to go home is staring right at him. As much pain as this world has brought him, deep down, Jonathan is going to miss this place and the friends he made.

"You can stay if you want. You are a hero. Your presence will never be unwelcomed; you are the savior of the Rebellion."

"I want to. But not now… I have to get back home. Maybe one day, I can come back."

"Very well," Skrinner says sullenly.

"Wait, I almost forgot," Jonathan says as he begins unclipping the belt that holds his sword.

"No, Jonathan. Keep it, you never know when you might need it."

"Are you sure? I know this sword means something to you."

"Nonsense, keep it. Hopefully, you never have to use it." Jonathan steps back and clips the belt back into place. He nods at Skrinner and then walks forward into the yellow window. The window crackles as Jonathan looks into the deep yellow of the portal. He steps forward and is engulfed in a sea of yellow.

168

Chapter Fourteen

Jonathan steps out into the Yellow Realm. It takes him a couple of seconds to recognize his surroundings and accept them as home. But once he does, Jonathan realizes that he is back in his room. It is night outside, and the house is dead quiet. A gust of wind comes howling in from his wide-open window. Jonathan walks over to the window and slams it shut.

He takes an extra moment to stare at the exact spot where he met Skrinner. Somehow, it all feels like some sort of twisted dream. However, the brown bag full of orbs and the sword he is carrying make him realize that it is all real. Jonathan takes a look around his room; everything still looks the same as it was when he left. He wants to check on his aunt and uncle but stops before he leaves the room. Jonathan goes to his bed and pulls out a black box that he uses to store his books about magic. He opens it, and a small puff of warm air rushes out. Jonathan has felt this before when around the books but never understood what it was. It was magic radiating from the books; that was what he always felt around them. The box is more of a chest and is big enough to fit his belongings. Jonathan puts the brown bag and sword inside. He takes a deep glance at the sword and bag before he shuts the box, hoping that he will wake up and that the sword and bag will still magically be there the next day. Jonathan eyes the sword and brown bag before shutting the chest.

His aunt and uncle are both fast asleep, and Jonathan has to fight with the idea of waking them up to announce his return. However, he begins to ponder. How long has he been gone? Hours? Days? Weeks? Months? His train of thought is interrupted by a sharp pain coming from his head. It takes him some time to figure out what it is. Then he remembers that the time difference between the realms would affect him for a while. Almost like an interdimensional jet lag, but much worse. He decides it is best to show himself to them in the morning. Jonathan tiptoes back to his room, which is cold with the wind that blew in from the outside world earlier. As he takes off his shoes, he still hopes that, when he wakes, the whole adventure will be revealed to have all been a dream. Jonathan throws himself on his bed, which seems to hug him back. He was worried it would take him some time to fall asleep, but as soon as his head hit the pillow, sleep carried him away. Jonathan is then engulfed in a sea of dreams.

Chapter Fifteen

Lava erupts from the volcano and fills the air with the smell of smoke and decay. The land is one straight from hell; the ground is covered in ash, and lava seeps through some cracks in the ground every now and then. A hooded figure stands, observing every person and creature that passes it in the marketplace. The land of Livingleh is one that many religious people would probably liken to Hell, but even Hell has a market. There are stands selling various foods, weapons, and artifacts. The hooded figure walks past every stand and every bystander and steps into the cold stone-built bar to the left. The music from the inside is loud, and the scenery is dark, with only red lights illuminating the dark club. The hooded figure walks up to a zed, a blue-skinned humanoid who is sitting by himself. The zed has a drink in his hand, his white clothes as clean as ever. His slick black hair makes his red eyes stand out even more. The hooded figure sits in the seat across from the zed.

"Vixen, I have come to confirm and pay for the mission."

"The credits?" Vixen motions with his free hand.

The hooded figure puts a gold coin on the table and slides it over to the bounty hunter.

"Such a handsome reward for the death of one boy…" the blue-skinned man says with a sinister smile.

TO BE CONTINUED…

About the Author

Mario A. Hernandez grew up in the South Bay of Southern California. He received his undergraduate education at California State Long Beach and then went on to the masters program at California State Dominguez Hills.

Mario is a contributor for various news sites but mainly Star Wars News Net. Mario currently works as a middle school English teacher, hoping to inspire his students to discover a love for literature.

www.ingramcontent.com/pod-product-compliance
Lightning Source LLC
Chambersburg PA
CBHW072133300726

48975CB00003B/1049